For William,
who knows that Vikings don't
have horns on their helmets.

Saving the Unicorn's Horn

Julia Edwards was born in 1977. She lives in Salisbury with her husband and three sons, and sometimes feels outnumbered.

Saving the Unicorn's Horn is the second book in *The Scar Gatherer* series, a sequence of seven adventure novels about time-travel.

To find out more, please visit: *www.scargatherer.co.uk.*

Also by Julia Edwards

Other titles in The Scar Gatherer series

The Leopard in the Golden Cage

The Falconer's Quarry

The Demon in the Embers

Slaves for the Isabella

The Shimmer on the Glass

The Ring from the Ruins

For adults

Time was Away

THE SECOND BOOK IN The Scar Gatherer SERIES

Saving the Unicorn's Horn

Julia Edwards

Published in the United Kingdom by:

Laverstock Publishing
129 Church Road, Laverstock, Salisbury,
Wiltshire, SP1 1RB, UK

First printed September 2014
Revised edition printed October 2019

Cover design by Peter O'Connor
www.bespokebookcovers.com

ISBN: 978-0-9928443-2-5

For more information about the series, please visit
www.scargatherer.co.uk

ACKNOWLEDGEMENTS

I remain indebted to my husband for his continuing support, and to my test readers for their eagle eyes and their enthusiasm for this sequel to "The Leopard in the Golden Cage". My particular gratitude, however, goes to Jan Bourne, whom I met at the Viking encampment at the Chalke Valley History Festival. She very kindly read my manuscript and corrected my mistakes, saving me from a couple of real clangers along the way! Any errors that remain are my own.

NAMES OF LUCY'S FAMILY

[and how to say them!]

Luiseach [LWEE-shak]	Lucy's proper name in this book
Aileen [Ay-LEEN]	Lucy's mother
Lokki [LOH-kee]	Lucy's father
Mattheus [MA-th-ee-as]	Lucy's eldest brother
Sorcha [SUR-ka]	Lucy's older sister
Peder [PAY-dur]	Lucy's second brother
Aine [AWN-ya]	Lucy's younger sister
Thorbiorn [THOR-bjorn]	Lucy's cousin

AUTHOR'S NOTE

The sharp-eyed among you may notice a piece of artistic licence in this book. The story takes place in late 926 and early 927, as defined by the death of a real person, Sigtryggr, King of Jorvik. However, Lucy's family possesses a narwhal horn, said to have been brought back from an expedition into arctic waters by Lucy's grandfather. In fact, the arctic region wasn't known to the Vikings until Erik the Red landed in Greenland in 982. I hope my readers will forgive me for bringing forward Erik the Red's discovery by about 100 years.

1

Joe stood at the foot of the ruined tower. He glanced around to make sure nobody was looking, then swung his St. Christopher on its chain and let it go. It flew through the air and landed with a tinkling sound beside the high stone wall. He looked around again. Nothing. Nothing had changed.

For the last two days, he'd been swinging it and dropping it whenever he saw a bit of stone that looked really old, hoping desperately that he could somehow magic himself back into the past. It was two months since he'd last seen his friend Lucy, in her Roman palace, but the memory of the time they'd spent together hadn't faded at all. In fact, he felt like he missed her more every day. On the night before his eleventh birthday, he'd lain in bed in the dark, wishing and wishing that he could slip through time and see her again. If he couldn't do that, the next best present would be Dad moving back home, so that they could be a normal family again, like before. Of course, neither thing had happened.

But when he'd arrived here in York with Sam and Dad, for the October half-term holiday, he'd had a really strong feeling that he would find a way of getting back to Lucy, even though he was hundreds of miles from where he'd last seen her.

He picked up the St. Christopher quickly before Dad came round the corner. He'd been told off once already for being careless with it.

"You were lucky to get that back after you dropped it at Fishbourne," Dad had said on the first morning, as Joe picked it up from the cobbled street outside the holiday apartment. "You might not be so lucky next time."

"Sorry." Joe put it in his pocket.

"I don't know why you don't put it on. It would be much safer."

But although Joe had bought a new chain to replace the one that had been lost, wearing the St. Christopher round his neck would have meant that he couldn't get it off easily when he wanted to drop it. And since that was the only way he could think of for getting into Lucy's world, he would just have to be more careful and not get caught.

"Look at that funny old building there," he'd said to distract Dad.

"Ah, yes!" Dad nodded. "That's Tudor. Those big, black beams are always a give-away. So along this street you've got Victorian, Tudor, Victorian again, then -"

"What about Roman?" Joe interrupted. "Wasn't York quite important in Roman times?"

His brother yawned. "I thought you'd given up on all that!"

"You're right, Joe," Dad said, ignoring Sam. "Roman York must be right underneath our feet. These cobbles are probably from a later period, but isn't it fascinating when you can see all the different layers of history in one place like this?"

Joe had agreed. It was just a pity, he thought, that the period of history he was most interested in was buried beneath all the rest.

He totted up now on his fingers. Since that conversation, he'd dropped the St. Christopher at least eight times without Dad noticing. But it hadn't got him anywhere.

"This is Roman, isn't it?" he asked, as Dad appeared.

"Certainly is." He read aloud from the sign on the wall. " 'Probably built in the third century, the Multangular Tower marks the west corner of the fortress.' " Dad looked at the stonework thoughtfully. "So that would make it something like 250AD."

Joe turned away to hide his disappointment. That was too late for Lucy. Even if she *had* somehow travelled all the way to York from Fishbourne - perhaps after her father had been put to death - she would still have been long dead by the year 250. And of course, if this was part of the fort, she was unlikely ever to have set foot here anyway. Why would a ten year old girl be wandering around among soldiers? No, this wasn't the right place either. It was incredibly frustrating!

"Shall we go into York Museum?" Dad said. "It's in the gardens just behind us."

"Can't we go to the Jorvik Viking Centre instead?" Sam asked. "I saw a poster. It looked really cool."

"It does seem to be very popular," Dad said. "There was quite a queue when we went past earlier. Let's leave it until later in the week, and hope that it's quieter."

So they spent the next hour looking around the museum together, peering at the objects in glass cases. Dad was just as enthusiastic as usual and Joe tried to lose himself in his stories like he'd always done. But now that he'd actually been there, back into the past, the stories weren't enough. He wanted the real thing.

By the time they had finished at the museum, it was late afternoon and already dusk. Mist crept up through the gardens from the river.

"Shall we find a café and have some cake before we go back to the apartment?" Dad said.

Sam groaned. "Can't we just go home now?"

Joe knew he was longing to get back and play on his new phone.

"No," Dad said firmly. "Let's go through the Shambles. That's another historic bit of York. It's very pretty and there's bound to be a café there."

As they walked back through the centre of the city, the streets were still busy. The lights in the shop windows were bright. Joe dug his hands into his pockets. Maybe it was worth dropping the St. Christopher one more time if he could, just in case.

The Shambles was a narrow street with old, crooked buildings down both sides. It was thronging with people. Joe paused, pretending to look in a shop window. Then, when a group of Japanese tourists were between him and Dad, he whipped his hand out of his pocket and dropped the St. Christopher on the pavement. It rolled into the gutter. Before he could catch it, it had fallen down between the bars of a drain.

He gasped and dropped to his knees.

All at once, his head filled with a hissing sound. The street was suddenly dim, as though all the lights had been switched off. He felt around on the ground. But there was no gutter and no drain, just a deep rut filled with muddy water. There was no pavement either. He'd done it! At last! He was back in the past!

He looked up, delighted. He was kneeling on a dirt track strewn with animal muck and straw, and mounds of rubbish like compost heaps. There was a smell of wood smoke, and another, much nastier smell in the air. He gulped, his excitement draining away instantly. It didn't look or feel like Lucy's time at all. Something must have gone wrong!

His fingers touched the St. Christopher. He fished it out of the puddle, relieved that at least he hadn't lost it, and went to wipe it on his trousers. They were not the jeans he'd put on this morning. Just as when he'd arrived in Lucy's world before, he was dressed for the time he'd landed in. He should have expected it, he supposed, but he still felt a jolt of surprise.

He stood up and looked at himself. On his feet were some kind of itchy socks and leather shoes like slippers. Through the sole of one, he could feel the lumps and bumps in the track he was standing on. Cold water trickled into the other where he'd just put his foot in the puddle by mistake. He grimaced and lifted it out, dripping. The hem of his trousers was wet too. They were long and loose, and above them was a woollen tunic that came down almost to his knees, pulled in at the waist with a leather belt. Over that, he wore a coarse cloak of a rusty colour, patched in places, and fastened at one shoulder with a kind of brooch. He examined it. It was silvery grey and circular, with a geometric pattern. Back in his own time, it would probably be priceless.

He fastened the St. Christopher round his neck and looked around. There were buildings on either side of the track, just as there had been in his own world, but they weren't the black and white Tudor ones hanging out over the road. These were thatched, with no upstairs, very narrow and close together, with tiny, dark passageways between them. As he stood there, a large rat ran out of one and scurried across the track right in front of him. It jumped over the puddle where his St. Christopher had fallen and disappeared down the passage opposite. Joe shuddered.

At that moment, a door opened in one of the buildings and a woman flung the contents of a wooden bucket out on to the track, spattering his ankles. The smell was abruptly even worse, of wee and something like rotten eggs and manure. Joe put his hand over his mouth. There was no doubt: he definitely wasn't in Roman times here. They'd had drains and clean running water, and paved roads. He shivered and pulled his cloak around him.

If this wasn't Roman, he told himself, then he would have to work out what period it was. He looked more closely at the buildings. The walls seemed to have been woven out of strips of bendy wood. He tried to remember the places he'd been to with Dad that had had buildings like this. Wasn't it called wattle, the woven stuff? He was sure it was usually wattle and daub, with mud or something stuck on the outside. There wasn't any kind of mud stuck on these walls. But in any case, it was the kind of thing you only really saw when they did reconstructions of very old buildings. So these must be ancient. Or rather, he must be a really long way back in the past.

He swallowed. If this was the Middle Ages, or even earlier, it could easily be a thousand years before his own time. Fishbourne had been even longer ago of course. But that hadn't really mattered because he'd had Lucy as his guide from the moment he arrived. This time, it looked like he was on his own. The thought of being so far back in the past without her was scary!

He shook himself. That was nonsense! It made no difference, how far back in time he was. He wasn't in his own world any more, and that was that. All he could do now was make the best of it.

He looked in through the open front of the building next to him, where the shop window had been a few minutes ago. Inside was a bench with tools laid out. On the wall hung what Joe recognised as a leather cow hide. A man was sitting on a stool behind the bench, bending over his work. Beside him stood a boy, watching.

"Last!" snapped the man.

The boy scurried across the room and brought something to him.

"Not that one! This is for a woman, not a giant! Bring the medium-sized last."

Joe took a step closer as the boy scampered away again. The man was making shoes like the ones he was wearing.

"Hurry up, will you? There's barely enough light as it is. We'll have to stop soon." Feeling Joe's eyes on him, the man looked up. "Did you want something, boy?"

Joe shook his head.

"On your way then. Your mother will be expecting you."

At his words, Joe felt something shrink inside him. His mum wasn't expecting him. She thought he was with Dad. He was *supposed* to be with Dad. And the worst of it was, Dad wouldn't even know he'd gone.

He set off slowly up the track, the way he'd been going with Dad and Sam in his own world. A boy went past leading a horse with large baskets strapped on either side, and then a girl with a goat. There were quite a few people about, though nothing like the crowds that had been in this street back in his own world.

In the workshops at the front of the other buildings, men and boys were tidying their tools. They all seemed to be leather workers, Joe noticed, and they were all finishing work for the day, drawing heavy drapes across, or lifting woven screens into place, to close up their workshops. The smell of wood smoke which had been in the air all along seemed to be getting stronger, covering the smell of filth and decay.

At the end of the street, Joe turned right. The next one was exactly like the first, the same thatched buildings crammed in together with workshops at the front, the same dirt on the ground, the same stench. He couldn't imagine ever getting used to the smell, but nobody around him seemed to notice it. People hurried by in the dusk. There was no electric light, he realised, nor even any windows in the buildings to cast light on to the track. But each time a door opened, there was a faint glow from within.

He wandered aimlessly through the town, not knowing what to do. Now and then, he had the feeling that he was walking along a street he'd been down before, but it was impossible to tell for certain. Presumably, this was still York, but there was no sign of the minster, and he hadn't come to any other landmarks either. There were no churches or other big buildings, only occasionally an empty space which might be a market place.

After a while, he found himself at a gateway in what must be the city wall. He looked out through the arch. The track he stood on led away across fields into bleak, open countryside. As he turned back towards the town, two men came and began to close the vast doors.

"Wait! Wait!"

Joe spun round. The voice was high and desperate.

The men paused. "Hurry up!" one called out gruffly. "You know the gates close at nightfall."

A girl clutching a large basket stumbled through the opening. Beside her trotted two wolf-like dogs. "I'm sorry," she panted. "I was further away than I thought."

The men shoved the doors shut behind her and

heaved two huge oak beams into position, barring the entrance. "By rights, you should have been out there all night," said the second man. "We can't wait for all comers."

The girl put down the basket she'd been carrying and swung a second basket off her back. The dogs waited patiently while she caught her breath. "I know. I'm sorry," she said again to the men.

Her voice sounded familiar, Joe thought. He frowned. In fact, she sounded just like Lucy. He stepped forward out of the gloom.

At once, he saw the dogs stiffen. The fur along their backs stood up and a low growling came from one of them.

He froze.

"What's the matter with you?" the girl said to the dogs, surprised. "It's alright," she called to Joe. "They won't hurt you."

"Lucy?" Joe shook his head in confusion. He took another step towards her.

In a flash, both dogs leapt at him, barking wildly. He saw their teeth, the whites of their eyes, their savage claws. He staggered away from them, shielding his head with his arms. At any moment, they would tear into his flesh.

But suddenly, the animals fell back, whimpering, as if they'd been hit by some invisible force. They scrabbled to get behind the girl's skirts.

"What was all that?" she shouted at them. She

ran forward to Joe, who was still cowering on the ground. "Are you alright? I'm so sorry! I've never known them do that before! I don't know what's got into them today!"

Joe let his arms drop. He was shaking. He tried to smile. "It's alright. They didn't touch me."

"Well, as long as you're not hurt." She straightened up. "I'm really sorry," she said again.

Joe looked up at her in the near darkness. She was wearing a long woollen dress with wide sleeves, and over it, a kind of pinafore, fastened at each shoulder with a pair of brooches like the one on his cloak. Her dark hair was wound up at the back of her head and she looked about the same age as him.

"Aren't you ...?" He broke off, hesitating, then began again. "You're Lucy, aren't you?" he said.

She paused in the middle of hitching her basket on to her back. "Not Lucy, Luiseach."

Joe got to his feet, watching the dogs in case they should decide to spring on him again. But they backed away. "You look just like someone else I know - Lucilia, the daughter of Lucullus." Joe fixed his eyes on the girl's face, hoping to see a flicker of recognition. But there was nothing. "You really do," he persisted. "You sound like her as well. I know it seems strange that we're both here now, but ..." His voice trailed off under the blankness of her stare.

"I don't know what you're talking about." She shrugged. "I'm Luiseach."

He stood in front of her. "Looeeshack?" he imitated uncertainly.

"That's right."

He shook his head. "I don't understand. You really don't remember me? I'm Joe." He watched her, but she didn't react at all. "I don't understand," he said again. "We met at Fishbourne. We spent hours together! You made me dye my hair with leeches, remember? Your voice is the same, your face is the same." He faltered. "Although your eyes ... I thought they were brown before, but now they're blue."

"Everyone has blue eyes in my family."

"Really?" He stepped back, defeated.

She bent to pick up the basket she'd been carrying in her arms. "I'm sorry. You've mixed me up with someone else. I'm not who you think I am, and my father isn't whoever you said either. His name is Lokki."

"What kind of name is that?" Joe asked meekly.

"Danish, of course!"

"And Luiseach? Is that Danish too?"

"Well, no." She smiled. "In fact, that's Irish. My mother was taken as a slave during a raid on Ireland years ago. My father brought her to Jorvik with him, then freed her and married her."

"Jorvik? That's the name of the Viking Centre. Are you a Viking, then?"

"I'm not a sea explorer, if that's what you mean. Though you could say my father is, or used to be.

Look, I really need to get home. My mother will be waiting for all this." She nodded to the baskets and began to walk away. The dogs cringed past her on the other side from Joe, and then loped ahead up the track.

Joe stood for a moment, bewildered. Then he ran to catch her up. "Please, Lucy - Luiseach - whoever you are! I've just arrived and I have nowhere to stay. I know the dogs didn't like me, but could you help me? Please!"

She stopped walking and looked him up and down. There was a long pause. Then she said reluctantly, "I suppose so."

2

"But you can start by helping me. Here, carry this!" The girl dumped her basket in Joe's arms. It was heavy.

"What's in here?" He peered down into it. "What are these?" He picked up a berry and squeezed it between finger and thumb.

"They're sloes. They're nearly over now. Those are just a few on the top. That's why I was late. I saw them on my way back."

"Back from where?"

She looked at him as though he was an idiot. "Collecting firewood and checking the traps." She jerked her head towards the basket she was carrying on her back. "I was lucky today. There's a hare in here. There could have been two, but the dogs weren't quick enough." She tugged on the leather straps at her shoulders, hoisting the basket further up her back. "And you're carrying crab apples, hazelnuts and a few walnuts. There are some haw berries too, if they're not completely squashed by the time we get home."

"Sounds like a feast!"

Once again, she looked at him strangely.

"Will I be able to stay at your house, then?" Joe asked.

"It should be alright. My mother will be pleased about the hare, so she probably won't mind having an extra mouth to feed this evening. If you're going to stay any longer though, you'll have to make yourself useful - earn your keep."

"Doing what?"

"The usual jobs, of course." She tilted her head to one side. "Where did you say you'd come from?"

"I didn't. But it's a very long way away." Joe found that he couldn't be bothered to explain again about his own world. It seemed so weird that she didn't know, when they'd been through all this before. He was absolutely certain that she was the same girl who'd become his friend at Fishbourne. And yet she clearly had no idea who he was. Perhaps he shouldn't really be surprised. After all, this was another place, hundreds of miles away, and another time too, hundreds of years later, he guessed, if they were now in the Viking age.

All the same, he couldn't shrug off his disappointment that she didn't remember him. He'd been longing to see her again. But it felt as though he hadn't been important enough to her to be worth remembering. That wasn't true, he knew. Lucy had been so happy to see him each time he'd appeared in her world before. No, this must be something to do with the way the time travel worked. Nonetheless, it made him uneasy.

"You speak Danish, though," she said.

"What?" He'd been lost in his own thoughts.

"I mean, it might be far away, where you come from. But it can't be that different if we speak the same language."

Joe didn't answer. He didn't know what to say. Last time, it had been Latin. Now it was Danish. But just like before, he felt as though he was talking normally, as he would to any of his friends back at home.

"Anyway," she said, "we're here now." She pushed open a door in a building just like the ones Joe had been looking at earlier.

He'd thought it was pretty dark outside, but it was darker still as Lucy closed the door behind them. It took a moment for his eyes to adjust to the gloom. He looked around. They stood in what he assumed was the workshop area, but it was empty of tools or materials of any kind.

"My father's away on the autumn raids," Lucy said, following his gaze. "He'll be back quite soon. When he's here, he works as a cooper, like everyone else in this street."

"A cooper?" Joe felt he ought to know what that was, but he couldn't remember.

"Woodworking. He turns cups and bowls, and

makes buckets, that sort of thing. He closes the business when he goes away and then starts it up again when he gets home."

"Is he away for a long time, then?"

"Yes, usually. Two or three months in late spring and early summer, and the same now. It depends how far they sail. If we have a chance later, I'll show you some of the things he's brought back. A lot of it gets traded straight away, but we keep a few things in case we ever need them." She dropped her voice to a whisper. "We even have a unicorn's horn!"

Before Joe could ask where the unicorn's horn had come from, or why you might need one, a curtain in front of them was pulled aside. The dogs slunk immediately past the woman who stood in the opening. She wore a long, woollen dress with a pinafore over it, like Lucy, and her hair was also uncovered. It was jet black.

"At last, Luiseach!" she said. "I was starting to worry! Who are you talking to?" There was a clear Irish lilt to her voice. Joe wondered for a moment whether she was speaking Danish with an Irish accent, or whether he was understanding Gaelic as well now. It didn't really matter, he decided.

From the room beyond the curtain, the fire flickered. Lucy bowed her head. "I'm sorry I'm late, Mother. But it was a good day. There was a hare in one of my traps." She swung the basket off her back and hauled the animal out by its ears. Joe was surprised by how big it was. He'd never seen one up close before, only rabbits. "And I met this boy while I was out," Lucy went on. "He collected the nuts and apples with me." She gestured to the basket she'd given Joe to carry.

Joe nodded, grateful that she was generous enough to pretend he'd helped her.

"He needs somewhere to stay tonight. Can he stay here?"

Joe curled his fingers tightly around the handle of the basket, waiting for Lucy's mother to answer.

All at once, he remembered how nervous he'd felt last time, standing in front of Lucy's mother at Fishbourne. In many ways, that had been different: Helena Calvina had been rich and powerful, and he'd been presenting himself to her as someone he wasn't. This woman looked tired. She looked older than Helena Calvina too. But then she'd clearly had a much harder life, without servants and slaves to wait on her. He looked at her as closely as he dared. She might be the same person. In any case, whether or not she was, it still mattered very much that she should let him stay.

"Does he have a name?" the woman said.

Lucy didn't answer. Joe realised she didn't know. He'd said it, but only in passing.

"I'm Joe," he said, wondering whether to add 'madam'. It would sound odd, he decided.

Lucy's mother nodded. "Short for Joannes, I presume."

Joe didn't correct her.

"I'm Aileen," she went on. "You can stay here for as long as you need to. My husband would want that. But you'll have to contribute to the household."

Joe felt a stab of alarm. "I don't have any money," he said.

Aileen stared at him for a moment, and then laughed. "I'm not expecting silver! You pay your way in labour - food, firewood, water."

Joe blushed. "Of course," he mumbled, holding out the basket of apples and nuts to her. At least this was easier, he thought, than the complicated story Lucy had dreamed up for him at Fishbourne.

Lucy's mother took the basket and beckoned them both through to the room beyond the curtain. Sitting on a stool was a boy a little older than Joe, whittling something with a knife. A tall girl stood stirring a large pot which hung above the fire, while a younger one was picking over a basket of sheep's wool on the floor.

"This is Joe," Lucy's mother said to them. "Joe, this is Peder, Sorcha and Aine." Seeing Joe's lips move as he tried silently to say the girls' names, she repeated slowly, "Sur-ka and Awn-ya." She smiled. "Most Danes find those names hard to remember. They're Irish, like Luiseach. The girls were named for me. The boys have Danish names like their father, Lokki. My eldest, Mattheus, is away with him now. It's his first raid." She spoke with pride, but Joe saw worry in her eyes. His own mother looked like that sometimes. He felt another pang of longing for her. She was so very far away. In fact, just now, she was completely out of his reach, since he'd never yet managed to get back into his own time when he wanted to. He pushed the thought of her away.

Aileen took the hare from Lucy and moved over to the fire, which provided the only light in the room. Shadows jumped all around the walls. "It should be my husband's last raid," she said, "as long as he comes back alive."

The boy whittling on the other side of the fire looked up. "It'll be his last raid if he gets killed too," he remarked.

"Don't say that!" cried the youngest girl.

The boy grinned. "Am I tempting the gods, do you think? He'll be fine, Aine. He's been raiding since long before we were born!"

Joe watched the boy. Peder, Lucy's mother had said he was called. From his voice, he could certainly be Lucy's twelve year old brother from before, Petrus, though his hair was now blond. Sorcha, on the other hand, was dark-haired like Lucy, and looked very much like Lucy's older sister, Sallustia. And the similarity between Aine and Lucy's little sister, Antonia, was unmistakable.

He turned this over in his mind. It was the same, and yet not the same. Lucy was the same girl he'd known before, and her family seemed to be the same as before too, with names that were parallel to the names they'd had in Roman times. The absent Mattheus must be Lucy's eldest brother, Marius, and her father, Lokki, must be Lucullus. But the time and situation they were living in was completely different. In the Roman age, Lucy's father had been one of the most important people in the country, and they'd lived in a palace with hundreds of slaves to serve them. Here, when he wasn't overseas on a raid, her father was a woodworker, and they lived in a house which seemed to have only one room besides the workshop.

There was someone missing, too. Tiberius. Joe felt the hairs stand up on his neck at the memory of him. He'd hoped never to see Lucy's adopted brother again. Perhaps Tiberius really had gone, as he'd said he would. But Joe was still half afraid that the older boy would step out of the shadows, with the same cruel smile and iron glint in his eyes.

He looked all around, staring deep into the darkness at the end of the room, just in case Tiberius was there. The dogs were lying on the floor with their heads on their paws, watching Joe warily. But there was no one else.

The room was long and narrow, and the walls were hung with drapes of some kind of heavy, dark material. In between, however, Joe could make out the wattle he'd noticed from the outside. It must be pretty cold in here in the winter. He wondered whether he would still be here by that time, and shivered.

The floor was earth, trodden down hard and spread with rushes and straw. Above his head, all sorts of things hung from the rafters: bunches of herbs, a large ham, and a rack of what looked like very stiff fish that he realised he could smell, even through the smell of the smoke. There were all kinds of tools as well that he couldn't identify. Above the rafters, the inside of the thatch was black and he could just make out a hole in the roof above the fire to let out the worst of the smoke. If it rained, the water must drip straight in.

Other than the fire, with the pot hanging over it, there wasn't much furniture. Along the two long sides of the room were wide banks of earth, held in by low, wattle walls. Joe wondered what they were for. Near the fire, two planks rested on a pair of trestles, acting as a table, and there were several small wooden stools, like the one Peder was sitting on. There was no sign of any beds.

"Right. Now that we're all here, shall we eat?" Lucy's mother had hung the hare by its ears from a peg on the wall and began ladling stew into wooden bowls which she set on the table. Joe hovered, not wishing to be the first to sit down. Lucy was unloading her firewood on to a stack beside the wall, and Sallustia - Joe corrected himself - Sorcha had fetched a tall, clay pot with a stopper and was pouring liquid into wooden cups.

"You'll need something to sit on," Aine said,

smiling shyly and holding out a stool to him.

"Thank you." Joe took it, but still didn't sit down.

"Anywhere you like," Peder said, as though Joe had spoken his uncertainty aloud. "We don't set places for dead ancestors in this household."

Joe blinked. He'd been afraid he might sit in Lucy's father's place, not in the place of someone dead. He sat.

Peder dipped his hands in a bowl of water and dried them on the cloth beside it. "Help yourself," he said, indicating the bowl. "And then there's stew." He pushed another bowl and spoon towards Joe. "And beer."

Joe rinsed his hands and then took the cup Peder held out. The liquid in it was dark. When he thought no-one was looking, he sniffed it.

"What's the matter?" Lucy said. "Don't you drink beer where you come from?"

He shook his head. "My father has it sometimes, but people don't usually give alcohol to children."

"What do you drink, then?"

"Water normally, or juice."

"You can actually drink the water?" Aine's eyes were wide.

"Of course!"

"Doesn't it make you ill?"

"No." Joe took a sip of his beer. It had smelled smoky and slightly sweet, but it tasted bitter. He hadn't really liked his dad's beer when he tried it, but this was much worse. He made himself keep a straight face though, glad of the practice he'd had eating snails with Lucy the first time he met her.

He scooped up a spoonful of stew. It was thin and greyish brown, with lumps of some kind of vegetables floating about in it. Rather than look at it too closely, he put it quickly into his mouth. This time, however, he was too late to stop himself from gagging.

He coughed to try and cover his reaction and stirred the stew around. The only thing he recognised for certain was leeks. There was something that tasted like carrot, but was greyish white, and there were no potatoes and no meat. From the taste of it, there was no salt or pepper either. What the lumps were, he didn't know. Turnip, perhaps, though he didn't know what that would taste like.

He took a deep breath and smiled at Aileen, aware that Lucy and the others were watching him. "It's a good stew," he said, taking another spoonful and managing this time to swallow it.

"It'll be better in a few days," Aileen said, "when the hare is ready to go in." She smiled back at him.

Joe began to eat steadily. If the food was going to be as bad as this every day, mealtimes were going to be an ordeal that he needed to get through as fast as possible. His stomach lurched, as he remembered how in Lucy's time before, he'd wished quite often that he could go home again. How was it that he always managed to forget that when he was back in his own world? The past was so much less comfortable: the food was weird, the beds were terrible, and several times he'd felt he was in real danger of getting hurt. And yet, almost the moment he got home, he wanted to come back. Perhaps that was what addiction was like.

He sipped his beer, hoping to get used to the bitter taste of it. For the last two days, he'd been trying and trying to get himself back into Lucy's time. Finally, he'd got what he wanted, even if it was Vikings rather than Romans. She was here and he was with her. All he had to do now was find a way to make the most of it. He just wasn't quite sure how.

3

Joe woke up the next morning feeling a good deal better. The wide, earth banks at the sides of the room had been spread with sheepskins last night, making a surprisingly soft, warm bed. They had slept in pairs: Lucy with Sorcha, her mother with Aine, and he himself with Peder.

To begin with, he'd lain rigidly still, afraid that when he slept, he might roll into Peder or accidentally cuddle up to him. But after a while, he'd realised it was much the same as sharing Dad's sofa-bed with Sam. The only difference was that he and Peder shared one large, thick blanket, rather than each having their own sleeping bag. When Joe awoke, the room was cold and he was glad of the warmth he'd had from Peder. Sleeping alone in a house like this would be rather chilly.

Lucy's mother and Sorcha were already up and dressed, conjuring the fire back to life. Without the light from it, the room was very dark. Joe lay on his back, looking up at the sky through the hole in the roof. Daylight filtered through chinks in the wall. He wondered what time it was, and went to look at his watch. It wasn't there of course, having disappeared with the rest of what he'd been wearing in his own world. It was probably around dawn, he guessed from the greyness of the light, which would make it something like seven o'clock. For a moment, he wondered whether they had changed their clocks here on the same date as at home. Then he realised that was a stupid question. More than likely, they didn't count the hours at all. Last night, they'd gone to bed soon after dinner, not long after it had got dark; and they seemed to be getting up now, as it got light. That, at least, was the same as it had been in Lucy's time before.

He frowned to himself. He had to stop thinking about the time at Fishbourne as 'Lucy's time'. This was Lucy's time now.

He sat up and pulled on his trousers and tunic over his linen undershirt and shorts. Peder groaned at the draught of cold air and pulled the blanket down around him.

"Time to get up, lazy bones," said Sorcha, coming over and prodding her brother. "You too!" She twitched the covers that lay over Lucy and Aine. There was a chorus of complaint. Joe grinned as he pulled on his shoes over the strange sleeve-like socks on his feet. He rubbed his arms, glad of the thickness of his tunic for keeping the cold out.

"Good morning," he said shyly to Lucy's mother.

"Hello, Joe. How are you?"

"Fine, thanks. Can I do something to help?"

"Could you milk the goat?" she said. Then seeing his face, she hesitated. "Or do you not know how to? Don't you have a goat at home? Or a cow? Or even a sheep?"

He shook his head.

"Never mind." She smiled. "Luiseach will show you how, and then you can do it. Come on, girl!" she called to Lucy. "Time to get out of bed!"

Lucy sat up, her hair tousled. She looked around sleepily. "Coming," she yawned.

Joe put on his cloak and went out through the back door. Behind the house was a long, narrow yard. He spluttered. It smelled disgusting out here, the same rank stench of rotting food and filth that had been in the street last evening. He hadn't realised how much better it had been inside with the smell of smoke covering almost everything else.

Near the house was a chicken coop and a lean-to shelter where the goat was tethered. Halfway down the yard was a sort of cubicle made from wattle, about the same height as Joe. It was arranged as three sides of a square, with the open side facing away from the house. It had no roof. Beyond it, down at the far end, was a pig in a pen, and beside that, a heap of what looked a bit like compost. A rat stood on top of the heap, twitching its whiskers. Joe picked up a stone and hurled it. The whole heap seemed to move, as a dozen or more rats he hadn't noticed vanished into their tunnels. The pig grunted and rolled over in its pen.

"What are you doing?" Lucy was beside him.

"Just scaring off a few rats."

She laughed. "That'll keep you busy all day long! Even the dogs can't keep them down. Not that we let the dogs burrow in there. They'd start eating the rubbish!"

Joe pointed to the wattle construction. "What's that?"

She looked at him intently. "You're not joking, are you?" she said after a moment. "You really don't know. It's the cess pit."

"Cess pit?" It took Joe a moment to realise what she was talking about. "Oh." He wrinkled his nose. "You mean where you wee?"

"You can, though there's a bucket for that in the house, because we keep quite a bit of the pee for washing clothes. Out here's mainly for pooing. There's no need to look like that!" She sounded indignant. "It's quite a good one actually. It has a plank seat, so you don't have to just squat over the hole."

"Right."

"Well where do you go when you're at home?"

"The bathroom, of course!"

"What? Like public baths?"

"No, not really. They're in our houses." Joe

sighed. There was no point telling her about bathrooms and toilets and sinks, and the clean water that came out when you turned on the tap. She couldn't possibly understand.

"Do you really wash your clothes in wee?" he asked instead. "They must smell horrible!"

"It's good for soaking away dirt and oil. Then we use soap before we rinse them."

"And what's that made from?" he asked, remembering the toothpaste and hair dye at Fishbourne.

"Wood ash mostly, or sometimes nettles, when they're in season. Anyway, the cess pit is one of our jobs for today."

"What?" The word came out as a squeak as Joe thought of having to shovel what was down the hole on to the heap.

"Collecting more moss," she said.

"Moss?" Her answer was so far from what he was expecting that he couldn't think what she was talking about.

She giggled. "For wiping your backside, you nitwit! We'll fetch some from the place I usually go to, near the river. Now, though -" she swung the pail she was holding - "it's time for milking." She put the bucket down beside the stool she'd brought out with her. "Can you pull down a few handfuls of hay from that net under the roof over there?" She pointed. "I'll hobble the goat. Then we can start."

Joe did as he was told, pleased with himself for guessing correctly that the hay was for the goat to eat. It was obvious too where he was supposed to put it. He gave the goat a cautious scratch between the ears as it buried its nose in the basket hung from the tethering post.

"What are you doing?" he asked.

"I just told you. I'm hobbling her." Lucy had looped a leather strap around both of the goat's back legs and pulled it tight.

"Doesn't that hurt her?"

"Of course not. It's only like wearing a belt. She's a kicker, this one. If we don't do this, she'll knock the bucket flying, milk and all, and then everyone will be sorry! Now, then." She pulled up the stool beside the animal and set the bucket down beneath its belly. "The udder has two sides," she said, "the right side and the left side. I milk the right side with my left hand and the left side with my right hand."

"Right with left, and left with right," repeated Joe, pretending to understand.

"So," Lucy went on, "I squeeze this teat with this hand. Then I let it go so that it fills up again, while I squeeze this one with this hand." She began to milk the goat. Joe watched, listening to the rhythmic squirt of the milk into the pail beneath. It looked quite easy.

"Your turn." She stood up.

"Don't I need to wash my hands or something?"

She shook her head. "Why would you do that?"

"I don't know. Hygiene, I suppose."

"What's hygiene?"

He sat down on the stool. "Forget it." He took hold of the goat's teats. They felt squishy, like the fingers of a rubber glove which had been filled with water, except that they were warm and slightly downy rather than rubbery.

"Not that one." Lucy grinned. "Those teats are both on the same side. You'll end up with one side empty and the other side still full. Here -" She guided his hand to the right place. "Now squeeze."

Joe did as she said. Nothing happened. "Her milk's gone! She's dried up! She must be frightened of me, just like the dogs!"

Lucy laughed. "She looks fine to me! You've just squeezed the milk back up inside her rather than out through the end of the teat." She bent down. "You need to close it off at the top by pinching it with your finger and thumb, like this." She showed him. "Then squeeze the milk down by curling your other fingers around it."

Joe tried again. This time, milk sprayed all over his leg.

"And you have to aim for the bucket!" Lucy was still laughing.

"It's alright for you!" he said crossly. "This isn't as easy as it looks!"

"I suppose not." She did her best to keep a

straight face as the next squirt shot over the top of the bucket on to the ground.

"Stop laughing, will you? You must have had to learn once!" Joe grappled with the pink sack which seemed to keep escaping from him.

"Easy on her!" Lucy sprang forward. "Don't pull. You'll hurt her. Just squeeze. And remember, if you get annoyed, she'll get tense, and then the milk won't come down." She stepped back again. "I'm sorry for laughing. I suppose I must have been shown what to do once. But it's so long ago, I don't remember it. Shall I leave you to have a go on your own for a bit?"

"Yes," Joe huffed. He'd be bound to do better without her looking over his shoulder and making fun of him.

For some time, he squeezed and squeezed the goat's udder. Sometimes the milk came through, sometimes it didn't. The sound on the bucket was certainly a lot less regular than it had been when Lucy did it, and the level of the milk was rising painfully slowly. Very soon, his hands ached.

Inside, he seethed. The trouble with coming into Lucy's world was that it was always one way - always him learning how to do something that she already knew how to do. It made him feel so stupid! And it wasn't even as though he could build on the skills he was acquiring. He thought of the hours he'd spent scraping letters in wax with his stylus under the fierce eye of the teacher at Fishbourne. When would that ever be useful again? And when would he ever be asked again to milk a goat? There was no point in learning all these things!

After a while, Lucy came out again. "Do you want to get her some more hay while I finish off?" she said tactfully. She sat down on the stool. Immediately, Joe heard the rhythmic swish of the milk squirting into the bucket.

"Here you are," she said after a couple of minutes. She motioned to him to take the pail and bent to unstrap the goat's back legs. "Don't worry," she said, seeing Joe's expression. "You can try again tomorrow. Now, while we're out here, we need to check in the hen house for eggs."

She unfastened the catch on the chicken coop and reached into the nest boxes. The chickens hopped down and flapped straight to the rubbish heap at the end of the yard. Joe watched them go. At least if he was asked to do this, he would know now where to find the eggs, and not panic about the chickens escaping.

"Will we have those for breakfast?" he asked, nodding to the four white eggs Lucy had brought out.

"No!" She looked faintly scandalised. "They're to sell or exchange for things we need, like flour or honey. We only eat eggs once a week, and that's not today."

They went back into the house. The fire was properly alight now, and the room smelled of smoke again. It occurred to Joe that he'd stopped noticing the stench outside while he'd been trying to milk the goat. Perhaps he would get used to this place after all, just as he'd got used to being at Fishbourne.

"Breakfast will be a good while yet," said Lucy's mother, seeing him looking around hopefully. "Peder's only just got back from the river with the water for the porridge. Perhaps you could chop some kindling."

Joe nodded and picked up the small axe she pointed to, before she could guess that this was something else he hadn't done before. While he was out in the yard again, trying to shave strips off the logs he'd found beneath the eaves, he wondered why the porridge was taking so long. His mother cooked it in about ten minutes at home and used milk rather than water, because she said it was nicer.

It was about another hour, he guessed, before they sat down in front of their bowls of lumpy, grey slop. He was ravenous. At home, he usually had breakfast as soon as he was dressed, rather than working for two hours first. But within a few chewy mouthfuls, his appetite had almost disappeared. The porridge tasted as grey as it looked, despite the honey Lucy's mother had added to sweeten it, and he had to force himself to eat it all. What was the point in milking the goat before breakfast, he wondered, if you weren't going to use the milk?

As he and Lucy set off through the streets, towards the gates out of Jorvik, he felt glum.

"So, we have to get moss and more firewood," she chirped. "And we'll check all the traps again." She grinned at him. "It's lovely not to have to carry everything myself for once."

Joe plodded along beside her and said nothing. The basket she'd used to carry the hare was strapped to his back instead of hers this morning.

"What's the matter?" she asked. "Did you want to go fishing with Peder instead?"

"No. I'd sooner be with you."

"Really?" She looked doubtful. "It doesn't seem like it."

"Sorry." Joe tried to pull himself together. "Everything's just a bit new for me, that's all. Where I come from, you see, it's really nothing like here at all. The food's different, the houses are different, pretty much everything is different."

Her eyes widened. "Will you tell me about it? Please! I love stories about other places. I've never been anywhere away from Jorvik."

Joe was tempted. This would be his chance to impress her, if only he could find a way of describing it so that she understood. It would make up for him not being able to milk the goat or chop the kindling, and for all the things he'd already said that she'd obviously thought were idiotic.

But just as he was about to begin, he looked up to see a boy a few years older than himself coming towards them along the street. The boy had curly blond hair and walked with a swagger. He was looking at Joe and Lucy with the kind of cocky satisfaction of a bully looking at his victim. Joe dropped his gaze to the ground. His heart thudded. That curl of the lip, the malice in the eyes - he was sure he recognised them. This boy might be blond rather than dark, but everything else about him was the same. Just as Peder was Petrus and Aine was Antonia, this had to be Tiberius.

He elbowed Lucy.

"What?"

"Who's that?" he hissed, still keeping his eyes averted.

Lucy looked up. Joe sensed her tense beside him. "Actually," she said loudly, "we need to go this way." She took Joe's arm and dragged him down a narrow alley which led away from the main track.

"Was that a good idea?" Joe whispered. "What if he follows us?"

"Just hurry up!" Lucy hissed back. "We don't want to run. But if we speed up a bit, we'll be able to lose him."

Joe quickened his pace to keep up with her. It was difficult to walk much faster without slipping and sliding in the muck and water that ran down the alley.

As they reached the end, he glanced over his shoulder. The boy had not followed them, but stood on the track at the point where they had turned off, watching. His mouth was twisted into a wide, cruel smile.

"Come on!" Lucy urged.

"It's okay. I don't think he's coming after us."

"All the same, we have to get as far away from him as we can, make sure he can't tell where we're going. Outside the city walls, there isn't much cover. And if he's waiting for us when we come back this evening, we'll be in really big trouble."

4

For the next ten minutes, they hurried along tracks and down alleyways, and even stumbled along one of the passages between the buildings, which was piled high with rotting rubbish. Joe was soon utterly disorientated.

"Wait for me!" he yelped, slipping into a puddle as he tried to keep up with Lucy. "I've no idea where we are. I'll never find my way back!"

She paused for a moment. "Jorvik's not that big," she said. "If you do get lost, just ask for Coppergate, or if you can't remember that, the street of the coopers." She looked up and down the track they had just come to, then darted out along it, and on to a wooden bridge across a river. On the other side, she turned immediately down another track. Despite what she had just said, it seemed to Joe that the city went on and on.

Finally, they came to a gate in the city wall, like the one she'd been coming through when he met her yesterday evening.

"Right!" She glanced over her shoulder. "Out through here, quickly. Then we should be fine."

The city was some way behind them before Lucy slowed down.

Joe hitched up the basket on his back, glad to be allowed to walk at a normal pace again. "Who was that boy, then?"

Lucy looked down at herself and then at Joe. Her pinafore and the skirts of her dress were streaked with muck and her shoes were filthy. Joe's trousers and shoes were the same.

"Oh dear," she said, pulling a face. "I think we'd better go to the river this morning, and wash the worst of this stuff off so that it can dry during the day. My mother won't be happy if I go back like this!"

"I don't understand, though. Why did we have to do that?"

"Jorvik has three gates in the city walls," she said. "It was obvious which one we were heading for, so it's quite likely Thorbiorn would have been waiting for us this evening if we hadn't crossed the river to a different one. He probably won't come now, because he won't know which of the other two gates to wait at."

"Thorbiorn, did you say?" Joe thought about the name. That could be an equivalent Danish name for Tiberius, he supposed. The other names hadn't been an exact match after all: Mattheus for Marius and Sorcha for Sallustia. But they were always sort of similar, just as the people themselves looked broadly similar, even if their hair or eye colour was different.

"He's my cousin," Lucy said. "But he hates my family. If he catches us this evening, he'll take everything we've collected today, and most likely give me a thick lip in its place."

"He'd hit you?" Joe was incredulous. "I would never hit a girl! Especially one younger than me!"

Lucy smiled ruefully. "Perhaps it's like you were saying before we saw him - things are different here to what you're used to."

Joe stopped to take a piece of flint out of his shoe. "So why does he hate you, if you're cousins?"

Lucy waited for him, flicking with a twig at a strand of something brown and slimy on her skirt. "It's a long story," she said.

"Tell me. We have all day, don't we?"

As they walked on again, Lucy began to explain. "For three generations," she said, "there was a feud between my father's family and another family. That was back in the homeland, across the water, before anyone ever came here. The story goes that it started because of a girl."

They had crossed a field, and were walking now along a belt of trees. Lucy paused to pick some nuts. Joe watched for a moment, then began to pick them from one of the other branches, throwing the soft green casing on the ground, as Lucy did.

"Put them in here." Lucy nudged her basket

towards him with her foot. "We'll keep your basket for the bigger things. Anyway," she went on, "this girl married my great-grandfather, which caused a big argument because the other family said that she'd been promised in marriage to their son."

"What did *she* want? The girl, I mean," Joe asked.

"She wanted to marry my great-grandfather."

"Why argue over it, then? Why would you fight to marry someone who didn't want to marry you?"

Lucy laughed. "You really are from another world, aren't you? The other family saw it as a matter of honour. Their son's bride had been stolen. So in revenge, they killed all my great-grandfather's horses."

"But that's awful!"

They finished collecting the nuts and went into the wood to find the first of Lucy's traps. "It got worse from there," she said. "One of my great-grandfather's brothers was so furious that he went and set fire to the other family's house, and burned it to the ground."

"No!"

"So then the man who'd been jilted in the first place killed my great-grandfather's brother."

Joe stared at her. "All because of a woman?"

Lucy nodded. "After that, it was a bloodbath," she said, matter-of-factly. "Someone from our family killed someone from theirs, they killed another one of ours, and so on. And it didn't stop with that generation either. My grandfather was killed, and one of my great-uncles. Then, when my father and his brothers became men, one of my uncles killed one of the young men from the other side."

Joe shook his head. "That's crazy!"

"To you, maybe. Anyway, the community decided that something had to be done. So it was agreed that one of my father's sisters would be married to the brother of the young man my uncle had killed."

Joe rubbed his forehead. "Let me check I've got this right. They linked the families by marrying your father's sister to the dead man's brother."

"That's right." Lucy bent down and moved the drift of leaves aside from the trap. "Empty," she said, covering it back over. "So that was supposed to put an end to it. And it worked, sort of. There haven't been any killings since. But the thing is, Thorbiorn was the son of the dead man. He was adopted by his uncle, who then married my father's sister."

"How old was he when this happened?"

"I'm not sure. It was before I was born. I don't think he was more than four."

"Do you think he even remembers his real father?"

"Maybe. Maybe not. That's the problem, though. He feels my family took his father away from him. He's never forgiven us."

"But your family is his family too, isn't it? His mother is your aunt."

"She's his adopted mother, though. His real

mother died in childbirth."

They walked out towards the open ground again. "Look, haw berries." Lucy pointed at a bush on the edge of the wood. "We'll pick some of those and put them in your basket for now, then tip them into mine later. Otherwise, they'll get squashed like the ones I picked yesterday."

Joe stood beside her, thinking about Thorbiorn and the feud while he picked the small red berries from amongst the thorns. Something similar had happened before, with Tiberius. Or at least, Tiberius had hated Lucy's family just as much.

"Leave the very small berries," she said. "They'll be really sharp, and we can't afford to use too much honey sweetening them."

"What about sugar?"

"What's sugar?"

"You know, the white stuff that looks like salt." Joe glanced across at his friend. Lucy's face was completely blank. "Never mind." He carried on picking. "So do you always have to keep away from Tiberius? I mean, Thorbiorn?"

Lucy cocked her head. "What did you just call him?"

"Forget it. I got muddled."

"Oh. No, not always." She dropped a cluster of berries and bent to pick them up from the ground. "It's just been the last few weeks, really. I mean, he's never liked us. That's always been obvious. But when his uncle and my father are at home, it's fine.

"Even when they were both away raiding in the spring, it was alright, because Mattheus was at home. He's a year older than Thorbiorn. There was a fight, but Mattheus won, and that was that. But of course, this time, Mattheus has been away as well." Her face was suddenly anxious. "Thorbiorn has already had all of Peder's fish a couple of times. Peder came home with a black eye the second time."

"What did your mother say?"

"She was angry, of course. The first time Peder came home empty handed, she went straight round to see my aunt, who gave the fish back. Peder thought that was why Thorbiorn punched him the second time. He pleaded with my mother not to go and see my aunt again." Lucy shrugged. "She still went, but that time, Thorbiorn had already sold the fish. So my aunt couldn't do anything anyway."

They moved along the hedgerow, still picking the haw berries and throwing them into Joe's basket.

"I'm scared of what he'll do if he catches me," Lucy said. "He's so much bigger and stronger than I am."

"It couldn't be that bad, though, could it?"

She emptied her hands and pulled at a long leather string which Joe hadn't noticed, hanging down beneath her pinafore. Attached to it was a small case carved out of bone. "Everyone carries a knife here," she said, opening the case and showing it to him.

"Wow! Isn't that dangerous?"

"It could be. We use our knives for cutting up food, or gutting fish, or for foraging like today, if we had to cut an animal free from a trap. So they do have to be quite sharp, otherwise they'd be no good."

Joe had a sudden vision of Thorbiorn towering over Lucy, a blade gleaming in his fist this time in place of the stylus he'd had before. Was this what people meant when they talked about history repeating itself? He gulped and blinked the vision away.

"It won't come to that," he said, more confidently than he felt. "At least, not while I'm around." As he said the words, a thought struck him. It was impossible to predict how long he would stay in Lucy's world each time. He might not be around for much longer, and if he wanted to return, he had to give her the key so that she could call him back.

"In fact," he said, "I'm going to give you something to help protect you." He unfastened his St. Christopher from around his neck.

"What's that?" She gazed at it. "It's beautiful! And where did you get such a fine chain?"

Joe smiled. "They're quite common where I come from." He put it round her neck and fastened the catch. "Think of it as a lucky charm."

"But I can't keep it!" Her eyes were wide. "It must be really precious to you!"

"It does mean quite a lot to me. But you need it at the moment. One day, when you've finished with it,

I'll have it back." He swallowed. It felt risky, giving the St. Christopher away like this. But it had worked last time, and it clearly had something to do with the time travel, since dropping it was how he'd arrived here.

She put up her hand and touched the little silver disk. Then she tucked it beneath the neck of her dress. "Thank you!" she beamed. "I promise I'll look after it!"

"Good. Now," he said, changing the subject, "I'm hungry. We didn't bring any lunch with us, did we?"

"Lunch? You mean something to eat? We don't have a meal in the middle of the day, just mornings and evenings."

"Really?" He was aghast.

She grinned. "I do usually find something I can eat while I'm out, though."

Joe tried a haw berry and made a face.

"Those are better cooked! You could eat a few of the hazelnuts we picked earlier. We can open the shells with my knife. Or we might find an apple tree."

"What about the one you went to yesterday?"

"That was crab apples, and anyway, it's on the far side of the city," she said, "through the gate we didn't go out of."

"How about rabbits? If we could catch one, we could cook it, if you know how to make a fire."

She shook her head. "Fire is really difficult

except when the weather's been dry for ages. Anyway, what's a rabbit?"

"It's like a small hare."

"A baby hare, you mean?"

"No, it's a different animal."

She looked at him blankly again.

"You know, I just can't get used to this," he said. "Even after last time!"

"Last time?"

"The time we met that you don't remember." He laughed at the look on her face. "All these things we eat every day where I come from, that you don't have - like potatoes and tomatoes and sugar. And rabbits! I thought rabbits were everywhere, whether you wanted to eat them or not! I still find it really strange!"

She frowned at him, perplexed.

"Never mind," he said. "Can I borrow your knife and open a few nuts?"

Somehow, the hours slipped past. They came to the river, and washed the mud from their clothes and shoes, which squelched on their feet while they collected moss. Joe ate too many sour apples so that his stomach grumbled for half the afternoon. And Lucy found a partridge in one of her traps and deftly twisted its neck before throwing it into Joe's basket. They collected wood for the fire, and more nuts and berries, and started to make their way back as the sun dipped in the sky.

As they came up to the city walls, Joe realised his friend had grown anxious again. While he was still chatting, she had fallen silent and was looking around them all the time. In the dusk, they slid in through the great gateway and crossed the city like shadows, keeping to the edges of the tracks. When she pushed open the door of her house, he heard her give a huge sigh, as though she'd been holding her breath for the last ten minutes.

Inside the house, it was just like the evening before. Sorcha, Peder and Aine were already there, Sorcha working this time at a large wooden frame that stood against the back wall. Her long hair was tied up at the nape of her neck, and she leaned toward the frame as she slid something flat between the taut threads. It must be a loom, Joe guessed. Nearer the fire, Aine stood beside the basket of wool she'd been picking over, drawing out yarn from the fleece, and spinning it on to a wooden spindle. In the flickering light, her eyes were fixed on the yarn, but she seemed not to see it, as though she were lost in a trance.

Lucy and Joe put their baskets down on the table. Although they had eaten quite a lot of the apples and nuts as they picked them, and hadn't caught anything as large as yesterday's hare, Joe was pleased to see that both baskets were still noticeably fuller than the previous evening.

"Well done, children," Lucy's mother said, sorting through the contents. "Luiseach, could you carry on draining this cheese while I deal with the nuts and fruit? Joe, could you take the moss out to the yard? You'll see a basket for it out there."

Outside, the sky was dark and there was no moon. As he came out through the back door, Joe thought he saw a movement in the shadows beside the goat shelter.

"Hello?" he called.

There was no reply.

He stared into the darkness along the end wall of the house. The goat stamped its hooves and blew air out through its nostrils. That must have been it, he decided. Just the goat. After walking home with Lucy the last part of the way, he'd started seeing danger where there wasn't any.

He walked purposefully down to the wattle screens. On the inside of one was a basket. He stuffed the armful of moss into it, pressing it down as it sprang back out.

Suddenly, there was an arm around his throat. He staggered backwards. His head was wrenched up painfully.

"Who's that?" he choked.

"I could ask you the same," snarled a familiar voice. "Who are you?"

Joe made himself relax all his muscles for a couple of seconds, as though he didn't have the will to fight. Then he twisted abruptly, digging his fingernails into the arm at his throat. Caught off guard, the other boy let go. Joe spun round to face him. It was Thorbiorn.

"I might have known," he muttered to himself.

"Known what?" The older boy stepped closer again. Even in the gloom, Joe could see his teeth.

"That it would be you. You don't change, do you?" Joe said. "What are you doing here?"

Although the other boy was quite a lot bigger than him, just as Tiberius had been, Joe found he was less frightened than he'd been before. Perhaps it was because he felt like he knew his enemy. He put his hand down to the scar on his thigh. Tiberius had managed to wound him last time, but *he* had won in the end.

"Who are you?" Thorbiorn snarled again. "You were with my cousin Luiseach today. But I haven't seen you before."

"I'm an old friend. My name's Joe." He watched Thorbiorn's face for any flicker of recognition. There was none. It was so strange to know all these people when they didn't know him.

"Well, Joe," the other boy said, with mock friendliness, "since you're here, you can do me a little favour."

"Why would I help you?"

"You don't have to 'help' exactly. I've come round to pick up these chickens."

"I'm not giving you a hand to get them in the basket. They're not yours!"

"Quite right. What you're going to do is take the blame for me!" Thorbiorn laughed sourly.

"No way!" Joe cried in outrage. Too late, he realised he'd backed himself up against the wattle wall.

Thorbiorn stepped quickly forward. His nose was inches away from Joe's.

"Hush," he crooned. In one swift movement, his hand was at Joe's throat again. "We don't want them to hear you inside, do we?"

Joe felt a cold, hard edge against his skin.

It was just as Lucy had feared. Thorbiorn had drawn his knife.

5

Joe stood completely still.

"It's very handy that you came out, actually," Thorbiorn murmured. "Better, really, than Peder."

Joe said through gritted teeth, "I'm not taking the blame for you stealing their chickens."

"It's alright." Thorbiorn shrugged. "I don't need you to agree. You'll be doing it, whether you like it or not. When it comes to the general assembly, they'll be much more likely to believe it was you who took the chickens, rather than me. I'm a member of one of the great warrior tribes, whereas you? Nobody knows you! You're just a wandering vagabond, who came into Jorvik to steal from honest townsfolk."

"Lucy and her mother won't think that! They won't believe I did it!"

"Lucy? Is that your pet name for my little cousin? I like it!" Thorbiorn sneered.

Joe ground his teeth together. "Aileen already knows you stole Peder's fish. She'll guess it was you!" He winced as Thorbiorn scraped the blade of the knife over his throat.

"Careful what you say!" the other boy hissed. "I could just slip with this. Save you the pain of having your little fingers cut off for the theft!"

Joe closed his eyes to hide his fear. The hissing sound seemed to spread out from Thorbiorn's voice into the air around him. It was growing louder all the time. He felt dizzy.

All at once, there was brightness behind his eyelids. He opened his eyes again. He was standing with his face pressed to the glass of a shop window, on the crooked street in York where he'd dropped his St. Christopher. He blinked, disorientated. It was dazzling! And it was so noisy and crowded!

He felt his breath rush out of him in a gasp. He'd got away! Thank goodness! A few seconds more, and he might even have been killed! He wondered whether Thorbiorn would have gone through with it. Perhaps not, but he was glad he hadn't had to find out.

He turned round. The crowd of Japanese tourists which had separated him from Dad and Sam was still trailing past.

"Let's go in here!" Dad called over.

Joe crossed the street to the café Dad had gone into. He felt like hugging him. It seemed so long since he had seen him. Of course, even in Lucy's world only twenty-four hours had passed. But it felt much longer. Meanwhile, no time at all had passed here. He should be used to that by now. But it still seemed incredible.

The café was warm and snug, with lamps on every wall. "We're so lucky aren't we," Joe said as he sat down, "to have all this light indoors."

Dad smiled, surprised. "I suppose so. It's only relatively recent, in the grand scheme of things. Even the gas lamps that were put in in the 1800s were pretty dim. And before that, mankind was more or less in the dark from dusk till dawn."

Sam rolled his eyes. "You two talk about the weirdest things! Why can't we talk about the kind of stuff that ordinary families talk about?"

"Like what?"

"I don't know. What's on TV, what's for dinner, that kind of thing."

Joe's tummy rumbled loudly, as though in answer to Sam's remark. He might have had lunch with Sam and Dad only a few hours ago, but his body felt like he'd eaten nothing but apples and nuts since the bowl of chewy, grey porridge this morning.

"Can I look in the cake cabinet?" he asked Dad.

"Of course."

Joe chose the biggest piece he could see, even though it wasn't his favourite kind. At dinner time, he had seconds of the stew Dad had made.

"Aren't you a hungry horse today!" Dad said, clearly pleased.

You've no idea! Joe replied silently. Out loud, he said, "What does hare taste like?"

"That's a funny question. I'm not sure I've ever had it." Dad put another dumpling on Joe's plate. "I'd guess it's quite gamey, like pheasant or venison, but I don't know that you've ever eaten either of those, have you?"

Joe shook his head. But he knew that if he got back into Lucy's world again, he would very likely end up eating one or another of those animals at some point.

For the next two days, however, there was no sign of him slipping through time again. He didn't mind. There was so much pleasure to be had from simple things like good food and soft chairs. So he went along happily with what Sam and Dad wanted to do. He felt much more relaxed too than he had done at the start of the holidays, when he'd been constantly hunting for places to drop his St. Christopher. He smiled at the thought of himself searching for Roman remains, when Lucy had turned out to be in another time altogether.

By Friday morning though, the novelty of being back had worn off. He kept thinking of his St. Christopher hanging round Lucy's neck. What had happened after he'd vanished from Thorbiorn's grasp? Had the older boy stolen the chickens? Had anyone caught him? Or would they assume it *had* been Joe, since he'd disappeared at the same time? It worried him that if he got back into Lucy's time again, he might find himself about to get his fingers chopped off, just as Thorbiorn had threatened.

But still he couldn't stop himself from wanting to be there again, to be spending time with Lucy, to be part of her life. It really was like an addiction. As soon as he got used to his own life again, he always started wanting to go back. It was so vivid, more real somehow than real life itself.

"We still haven't been to the Viking Centre," he said over breakfast.

Dad looked up. "I'm afraid the queues have been terrible every time we've gone past."

"I think we ought to go all the same," Joe persisted. "Sam wanted to, didn't you, Sam?"

His brother nodded. "It said on one poster that it has the sights, sounds and smells of Viking life."

"Oh no! I hope not!" Joe said with feeling.

His brother stared at him. "What? Why not?"

Joe turned red. He'd spoken without thinking. "I'm guessing it would smell disgusting," he said, to cover his mistake.

"How would you know?"

"I wouldn't," he lied, and got up from the table to rinse his bowl. "I'd like to go, anyway. Please, Dad."

"Alright, since both of you want to." His father smiled.

As they walked through the streets of York, Joe looked around for any sign of Lucy's time in the buildings around him. They might well be on the same ground he had walked on with her. But of course the timber and thatched houses had disappeared hundreds of years ago, and the wooden bridge across the river had gone too. He couldn't even work out whether the street layout was the same.

Dad wasn't joking about the queue. They shuffled along for nearly an hour as it snaked back and forth outside the building. Joe kept his spirits up with the thought that it was worth the wait just to have the chance to stand on real Viking soil again. After all, this was the place where they'd done the famous excavation and found all the Viking remains. Better still, the Jorvik Centre turned out to be on Coppergate, the actual street where Lucy had lived. He couldn't help hoping that he might manage to slip back into her world somehow. It felt like fate, even though he knew that it didn't necessarily work like that. Tomorrow, they were going home, and then he would be over two hundred miles away. Surely, he was much more likely to find the way back when he was in the right place.

Eventually, they reached the front of the queue, bought their tickets, and went down the stairs. Joe tingled with excitement. Perhaps Lucy's house would be recreated here and there really would be a door he could go through that would take him back in time.

At the bottom of the stairs, he stopped. Over the heads of all the people already in here, he could see a huge video screen showing an information film. Around the sides of the room were brightly lit cases of objects which had been found during the excavation, interspersed with touch-screens offering more information and short films. He looked down. Beneath his feet was a glass floor, and underneath that was some kind of reconstruction of the dig, also lit up.

He shook his head at his own surprise. It was extremely well presented, and yet it wasn't at all what he'd been expecting. He tried to work out what he had imagined. Firelight in the darkness, perhaps, like being inside Lucy's house. And being able to stand on the actual soil where Lucy had stood. But of course, no visitors' centre could possibly do either of those things. You couldn't have a real fire in a building like this, and without electricity, nobody would be able to see anything. As for standing on the soil itself, it would have been worn away years ago with the thousands of feet that tramped through all the time. It was ridiculous to feel disappointed!

"Look at this!" Sam called out. Joe wove his way across the room to his brother, still trying to adjust in his mind. "These interactive things are cool. Look!" Sam touched a screen and started a video. "There's another one over there, as well." Without waiting to watch even thirty seconds of the film he'd started, Sam disappeared across the room.

Joe stood and watched the video, then looked around to see where Dad had got to. He was watching the film on the big screen. Joe squeezed through to stand next to him. As long as he forgot any idea of getting back into Lucy's world, there ought to be plenty of useful information he could get out of this visit.

"When did the Vikings come to York, then, Dad?" he asked, as the film came round to the beginning again, and his father moved away to look at the displays.

"In 866," Dad said. "They settled here permanently in 876. It was known as Jorvik, which is where the centre gets its name from."

Joe scratched his head. "So what happened in all that time between the Romans building Fishbourne and the Vikings settling in Jorvik? That's 800 years."

"Well, the Romans were here in Britain, in York too, until just after 400. And then comes the bit that we call the Dark Ages."

"Is that because there wasn't any light?"

Dad laughed. "No! If that had been the case, the Dark Ages would have gone on for much, much longer! No, it's the period from about 500 to 1100, so it includes the Vikings. We call it the Dark Ages because we don't know very much about it."

They drifted along the cabinets, pausing to looking at some of the artefacts. There were knives among them, the handles gone and the blades dull and chipped here and there along what would once have been the sharp edge. How odd, Joe thought, that one of these really could be the very same one Thorbiorn had held to his throat just a few days ago! Hundreds of years buried in the ground had robbed them of their menace.

"So were the Anglo-Saxons in the Dark Ages, then?" he asked, as they moved along.

"Yes, though first there was a lot of fighting between different tribes after the Romans left. There wasn't really anyone in charge, you see. So there were the Britons who were here already, who we sometimes call Celts, and there were the Picts in the north. The Angles, Jutes and Saxons came over from Scandinavia and Germany, invited by the king of the Britons to help him beat back the Picts."

"And then they took over?"

"Basically, yes. It's hard for us to imagine, but it must have been a very violent time. The Angles and Saxons helped the Britons, and then turned on them and pushed them back into Cornwall, Wales and Scotland, and across the channel to Brittany in France. If you think about it, those are places where you might hear a different language being spoken, and where the people have their own regional identity, even today."

Joe grinned. "Never call a Welshman English!"

"Quite so! Big mistake!" Dad pretended to punch Joe. "I should never have let your mother lure me away from my Welsh forebears! Anyway, the language we speak now goes back to that time. And so do a lot of our place names, even the ones we think of as Roman, ending in 'chester' or 'caster' or 'cester', like Winchester and Doncaster and Leicester."

"So it wasn't the Romans who did that?" Joe said. "I was wondering about that before. They called the town near Fishbourne Noviomagus. But we call it Chichester."

"That's right. That'll have been the Anglo-Saxons."

"And what about York? I thought this was a Roman fort?"

"It was, but it was Eboracum to the Romans, and then Eoforwic before the Vikings came. They changed the name to their own version, Jorvik, and that eventually became York."

They stopped to look at a shoe in one of the glass cases.

"Imagine wearing that," Dad said. "You'd feel every stone in the ground through the leather sole. That would be so uncomfortable, don't you think?"

I don't have to imagine it, Joe thought. *I know.* "You'd probably get used to it," he said, and then wondered whether that was true. Had he stopped noticing it really? Or was it just that everything in Lucy's world was so different that his brain ignored the little things and focused on the important stuff?

"Maybe." Dad raised an eyebrow.

"So, did the Vikings come after the Anglo-Saxons?"

"No, they were around at the same time. The Vikings started raiding England, looting monasteries and churches, and terrorising whole villages. The

Anglo-Saxons kept having to fight them off, and when that didn't stop them, they tried paying the Vikings to stay away - it was a lot of money, called *Danegeld*. But not surprisingly, the Vikings thought that was a wheeze and came back asking for more. Eventually, the Anglo-Saxons agreed that the Vikings could have a large area in the north of England, including York, known as the *Danelaw*, while the Anglo-Saxons kept control of south and central England."

"And the people who settled here were Danish, were they?" Joe thought of Lucy's family. She had said they were speaking Danish, and the boys had Danish names.

"Probably. But possibly also Norwegians and Swedes too. I'm no expert on that."

At that moment, Sam reappeared. "Oh good, you're in the queue."

"The queue? Are we? What for?"

"There's a sort of ride over there. That's what all these people are waiting for. The cars keep coming through so we won't be long." He went and stood beside Dad.

Joe fell silent, not wanting to ask any more questions in front of Sam. As they moved forward, he tried to digest what Dad had said and what it meant for Lucy. Had she just jumped forward in time by 800 years, or had she lived other lives in between, that he hadn't seen? In late Roman times, say, after the palace at Fishbourne had burned down? Or as a Saxon coming over from Germany with her family? Or a Celt, forced to flee into Scotland or Cornwall? There was no way of finding out. There was no point in asking her when he next saw her either, since she didn't remember the other life that he *knew* she'd had.

They reached the front of the queue.

"Are you ready to experience the sights, sounds and smells of the Viking age?" asked the attendant, as they climbed into the waiting car. "Press the Union Jack button for commentary in English and let us take you back in time." He pulled down a bar across their laps.

The car moved slowly along its rails into a reconstruction of a Viking street.

Joe felt his pulse quicken. This was supposed to be the street where Lucy had lived, and it did look sort of similar. Surely, it couldn't be coincidence that he was here on the exact same spot, of all the places he could have been in York! He leaned forward and looked keenly at the figures and houses around him. There must be a way to get back to her. Fate had brought him here for a reason.

He just had to find the right moment.

6

Sam was still brimming with enthusiasm for the Jorvik Centre while they were having lunch some time later. "That skeleton at the end of the museum was awesome!" he said, for the umpteenth time. "Sixteen wounds! Get that! The axe in his leg, the stab wounds, the wounds on his arms while he was trying to defend himself with his sword! And then the execution wounds! It was so cool!"

Joe was about to tell his brother to shut up, but Sam had fortunately stopped talking. Perhaps he'd finally realised how horrible it was to get so excited at the thought of someone being murdered. What was the matter with his imagination, Joe wondered. It had been obvious while they were looking at the skeleton that his brother wasn't seeing this poor man in the last minutes of his life.

Joe had pictured him quite clearly, kneeling on the ground. The sixteen injuries on the skeleton didn't include cuts that had only gone into his flesh, so blood had probably been streaming out of him. He'd knelt there in front of his enemy, knowing he was about to die, just waiting for the blow to the back of his head that was going to end his life. What were the last thoughts that had gone through the skull they were looking at? He might have been as young as eighteen, the archaeologists said. Joe felt sure he'd been thinking of his mother. He must have been full of grief that he would never see her again. And surely he'd been frightened too at the thought of his own death. Joe knew he would be. He'd found it both horrifying and terribly sad.

Of course, he'd been feeling rather sad anyway. They'd been right at the end of the museum by then and he hadn't found a way to get back to Lucy. There had been no possibility of climbing down from the car on the ride because the bar was so tight across their laps. And though the reconstruction of the Viking street had been interesting, and reasonably accurate, the waxwork figures weren't real people. The voices recorded for them spoke a language he didn't understand, and the narrator kept talking about Coppergate as the street of the cupmakers rather than the coopers, as Lucy had called it.

As for the smells of Viking life, there had been a faint waft of something now and then, but nothing like as bad as the real thing. On balance, he thought, that was probably just as well. He found he was smiling. Even *he* couldn't bring himself to long for the stink of Lucy's Jorvik!

Lying in bed that night, however, he thought hard about Lucy. He had once found himself whisked into her time while he was waiting to go to sleep, so it wasn't impossible. A few times, he thought he heard the telltale hiss that always seemed to fill his ears as he slipped between worlds. But each time he held his breath to listen, it turned out to be a distant car, or the wind, or nothing at all. He wished he'd told Lucy how he thought the St. Christopher worked, by her holding it and thinking of him at the same moment as he thought of her. But he'd just put it round her neck and not said anything about it.

Eventually, he fell asleep.

Dad woke him and Sam early the next morning. "Get dressed, please, and sort out your breakfast. We need to pack the last few things and do a basic clean-up before we leave. Our train is in two hours."

Sam moaned sleepily. Joe sat up. Two hours. In two hours, they would be gone from York.

While he helped Dad with the washing up, he could feel a growing sickness in his stomach. He wasn't ill, he knew. This was how it always was when he was unhappy about something. He tried to work out whether it was because it was the end of the holidays - and therefore the end of their time with Dad - or whether it was because he felt like he was leaving Lucy. That was silly, of course. You couldn't leave someone who wasn't there.

They arrived at the station with ten minutes to

spare. Joe sat hunched up between Dad and Sam on the platform bench. He could feel the cold metal of the seat through his jeans. None of them spoke. Dad was reading the paper and Sam's eyes were glued to the screen of his phone while his thumbs stabbed at it with frantic little movements. Joe stared miserably into space.

After a while, there was a whispering along the rails. He looked up. The train was just coming past the signal points outside the station. He stood up.

Dad folded his paper and got to his feet. "Come on, Sam," he said. "We don't want to leave you behind."

Sam stood up, not taking his eyes off his phone.

The train swung along the track and in beside the platform, creeping along until it came to a stop.

I wouldn't mind leaving you behind, thought Joe. *You're so boring, wrapped up in that thing every second you're allowed. Given the choice between you and Lucy, I'd leave you behind quite happily and take her.*

There was a hiss as the doors opened. Joe took hold of the handle of his pull-along bag. The hissing grew louder and louder. He swayed, feeling slightly dizzy, and steadied himself on the nearest thing.

It was the wattle construction in the yard behind Lucy's house. He screwed his eyes shut and then opened them again. The station had completely melted away. The smell of rubbish and decay was in the air again, and the scent of wood smoke from the roofs above. He waited, bewildered, for the dizziness to pass. The trouble with the way the time slip happened was that it never seemed to be when he was ready, so he always felt as though he was caught out.

He rubbed his eyes and tried to work out what time it was. It was only just light, so it must be quite a bit earlier than it had been in his own world. That was another thing about moving into Lucy's world from his own: it seemed as though time passed at a different rate, so the time of day and season only matched when he first went. When he'd gone back to Fishbourne the second time, it had been night at home but day there. And in Lucy's world it had already been autumn where it was still summer in his own time.

Here, now, it was presumably around dawn, and much colder than at home. Only four days had gone by in his world, but it seemed that weeks or even months might have passed here. He patted his cloak, to see if he was wearing any extra layers, but his clothes felt the same as before. He shivered.

The only thing he could rely on was that he would reappear in the same spot he had disappeared from. That was how it had been before, and again this time, he was standing exactly where Thorbiorn had pinned him, with his back against the wattle. He glanced around to be sure that the older boy wasn't still here. But the yard was empty.

He pulled his cloak tight around him and stepped away from the wattle screen. The pig pen down at the end of the yard looked as though it was empty, but he could hear a gentle clucking sound from the chicken coop up near the house. Perhaps Thorbiorn had been so alarmed by his disappearance that he'd decided to leave the chickens. Joe very much hoped so.

The back door of the house opened. He froze. If this wasn't Lucy coming out, it might be better to hide. But it was already too late: if he moved, he would draw attention to himself. He would just have to stand very still and hope the person wasn't heading for the cess pit right behind him.

A girl stepped out. Joe peered at her. She carried a bucket in one hand and a stool in the other, and she had a hood over her hair. It looked like Lucy, going to milk the goat, but he had to be sure he hadn't mixed her up with Aine or Sorcha before he approached.

He watched her fetch hay for the feed basket, and then fix the strap around the animal's back legs. Then she sat down on the stool, making soothing murmuring noises. It was definitely her.

"Pssst!" he whispered. At once, she turned her head. "Pssst!" he whispered again. "It's me, Joe."

She spun round on the stool. The goat stamped at her sudden movement. "Joe?" Her eyebrows were drawn together and she looked anxious.

Joe walked quietly up the yard towards her.

"Hello, Lucy," he said softly.

"Lucy?" She looked confused. "Oh yes, that's what you called me before. Where did you spring from?" She was still frowning.

"I came back as soon as I could," he said, ignoring the question. "Sorry I didn't manage to say goodbye before I went."

She shook her head. "I don't think it's a very good idea for you to be here."

"Oh." He knew he sounded crestfallen.

"At least not until we've had a chance to talk."

"Okay."

"Okay?"

"I mean alright. But can't we talk while you milk the goat?"

"Someone might come out. You can meet me at that end of the lane later on." She gestured past the house. "After breakfast, when I go out for firewood."

"Alright. How do I get out there from here?"

"Well how did you get in?"

"I just ... never mind. Will I be able to squeeze down the side of the house?"

Lucy pulled a face. "If you don't mind what you tread in!"

Joe grimaced. But the alternative would be to try and climb over the fence to the next yard, and then the next, and risk breaking the fences or getting caught. He would have a hard time explaining what he was doing on someone else's property. And if he was already suspected of stealing chickens, as Thorbiorn had intended, that could be a very bad move.

"Right." He tiptoed towards the narrow passage between Lucy's house and the neighbours'. "I'll see you down there later on."

It seemed a very long time until Lucy reappeared. Of course, it might easily have been as much as two hours, he realised, judging by how late breakfast had been last time he was here. Joe had thought he wasn't hungry, certainly not for Aileen's lumpy porridge. But his stomach started to rumble while he waited. At home, it would be time for elevenses.

He drifted around. There wasn't any kind of bench or low wall he could sit on, and the ground was still filthy, even though the water in the ruts was frozen. Around him, craftsmen opened up their workshops for the day, many of them moving their benches out into the street to make the most of the dull daylight.

At last, he saw Lucy coming towards him, carrying the same baskets she'd had before. He was about to speak, but she shook her head and motioned to him to follow her further away from the house. They were at the gates of the city, where he'd first seen her, before she stopped to let him to catch her up.

"You decided to come back then," she said, as they walked together through the gates out into the countryside beyond. "We thought you'd gone." She sounded reproachful.

"I'm sorry. I'm sure you did. I can't seem to help it."

"Right." It was clear from her voice that she didn't believe him. She shrugged her shoulders, as though she didn't care anyway.

"I didn't take your chickens though," he said.

"Why would I think you did?"

"Didn't they get stolen?"

"No."

Joe sighed in relief. "That's great!"

She looked at him. "I don't understand you! First, you vanish into thin air. And then, when you suddenly turn up again, you're really happy about something that didn't happen!"

Joe laughed. She was right, in a way. "That night," he said, "your mother sent me out to the yard with the moss, remember?"

"Yes, and you didn't come back. We even lit a reed taper and took it out there to see if you'd fallen into the cess pit. But you'd gone, without bothering to say goodbye or thank you, or anything!"

"Thorbiorn was out there, when I went out."

He saw her muscles tense instantly. Her eyes were fixed on a spot just ahead of her, but he could see that he had her full attention.

"He was about to steal your chickens."

"And you stopped him? That was brave!" she exclaimed.

"Not exactly." Joe was reluctant to correct her, but she had to know the truth. "He said he was going to do it, but he would make sure that I got the blame. I said I wasn't going to let that happen, and he put a knife to my throat."

Lucy's eyes were like saucers. "What happened then?"

"I disappeared." He blushed. It sounded so lame.

"You disappeared," she repeated slowly. "What do you mean?"

"Exactly how it sounds. One minute, I was standing there in the yard, with Thorbiorn's blade on my neck, and the next minute I was back in my own world. I guess Thorbiorn was left looking at empty space."

She stopped walking. "Are you talking about magic?"

"Sort of, I suppose." Joe turned to face her. "I don't really know what it is, but magic would be one way of describing it."

She brightened. "Can you make spells then, and put curses on people?"

"No. It's not that kind of magic. And like I said, I can't control it."

Her face fell.

Joe felt a twinge of regret that he was disappointing her. "I told you when we met that I came from a long way away. Well, it *is* quite a long way away geographically. But what I really meant is that it's another time in history."

"Another time? Like night time?"

"No, another period. Like there were the Romans and now there are the Anglo-Saxons and the Vikings."

She looked completely baffled.

"You know about history, yes?"

"You mean the stories in the sagas about our ancestors?"

"Not exactly. I was thinking more of the history you learn in school."

"What's school?"

Joe took a deep breath. This was even more difficult than he'd expected. "It's where children go to learn things, like reading and writing, and numbers." He watched her for any sign of understanding. "Never mind. Anyway, what I'm trying to say is that I'm from a time that hasn't happened yet in your world."

"You mean tomorrow, or next summer, or something?"

"Sort of, only much further away. If you think, in ten years time, you'll be a grown up. Well, where I live is over a thousand years from now."

"How many is a thousand?"

"Argh!" He ground the toe of his shoe against the path in frustration. These conversations with Lucy always came to a dead end because the gap between their worlds was just too big. In fact, it seemed to be worse this time round, because it looked like she had no idea about anything. At least in Roman times, she'd been rich enough to be getting some kind of education, so she hadn't been asking what school was or how many was a thousand! He sighed. When there was something he didn't understand in her time, he could find out about it on the internet or in a book when he was back at home. But she would never have any idea about his life.

He looked up. She had walked on ahead of him. Although she was still carrying the big basket on her back, he could see that her shoulders drooped.

"I'm sorry," he said, as he caught her up. "I knew it was going to be hard to explain."

She didn't answer.

"Let's forget it, shall we? Give me one of those baskets to carry."

Without looking at him or slowing down, she snapped out her arm with the basket she carried in front of her. He took it and waited to see if she would say something. But it was clear, she had decided not to speak to him.

For a while, they walked in silence. A bitter wind blew across the open countryside. Joe shuddered and tried to think of a way of mending things with Lucy. There was no way of knowing how long he would be here, and he didn't want to waste time arguing.

"How are things with Thorbiorn now?" he asked at last, hoping that the mention of their shared enemy

7

"Trouble? What kind of trouble?"

Lucy led them off the track into a copse, and began to pick up dead branches which she broke into shorter lengths. "Well, it's funny you should say that Thorbiorn was in our yard that night, about to steal our chickens." She flicked the sticks into the basket on her back.

"Why's that funny?"

"Because not long after, Thorbiorn's chickens - that is, the chickens his family kept - they got stolen. Thorbiorn claimed it was Peder. He swore he'd seen him do it. He reckoned Peder was getting his own back for the fish."

Joe put his basket down and began to collect brushwood. Crystals of frost clung to the wood where it was damp. He rubbed his hands against his cloak to warm them. "What did Peder say?"

"He said it wasn't true, of course."

"Did your mother believe him?"

Lucy nodded. "She knew as well that he

wouldn't have been brave enough to do something like steal chickens."

"Not brave enough? Don't you mean too honest?"

"Not really. It's not dishonest, is it, if someone's taken your fish already? It would have been fair enough for Peder to take a chicken or two in exchange."

Joe threw an armful of sticks into his basket and looked over at her. "It's not exchange though, is it? It's revenge! I can see how you might think that was fair, but two wrongs don't make a right."

Lucy stuck out her jaw. "Actions should have consequences," she said fiercely.

"But isn't that how a feud starts? He does something, so you do something, and then he does something worse, and then you match that. And it all ends up like you were saying before, with people killing each other!"

"Well anyway." Lucy turned her back and picked up a log for her basket. "Peder didn't do it, and the Thing agreed he wasn't guilty."

"What thing?"

"The *Thing*!" She shook her head at his ignorance. "The general assembly, where everyone meets to decide on making laws, or voting for new leaders, or punishing crimes."

"Ah." Joe nodded. "Thorbiorn said something about that. He said the assembly was bound to believe it was me rather than him who'd stolen your chickens, because nobody knows me. He said my little fingers would be cut off." He felt goose-bumps rise on his skin at the thought.

"It's possible," Lucy said seriously. "That *is* one of the punishments for stealing, though it would be pretty harsh for such a small thing. They normally do that to bandits, if they're not flogged or scalped."

Joe winced. "What would have happened to me, then?"

"Your family would probably have been made to pay a fine."

"But I have no family here, and no money! I only have the clothes I'm wearing! Nothing else."

"In that case, you'd have become a slave. That's what happens when people can't pay."

"I thought you didn't have slaves here! Didn't your father free your mother from slavery?"

Lucy broke a long branch beneath her foot. "He did. But plenty of other families keep slaves." She didn't seem concerned.

Joe frowned. He'd got an idea of what it might be like to be a slave when Lucy was living in Roman times. The chances were, it wouldn't be any better here.

"Of course, you could have asked to go through an ordeal to prove your innocence," Lucy said cheerfully.

"Such as?"

"Carrying a red-hot poker in your hands. Or picking stones out of boiling water."

Joe was horrified. "How would that prove I was innocent?"

"They bandage your hands for three days afterwards and then check the wounds. If they're starting to heal, you're innocent. If they're festering, you're guilty."

"But that's barbaric!"

Lucy shrugged. "Or there's cow grappling."

"What on earth is that?"

"They catch a wild cow and grease its tail. Then they grease your shoes and you have to hold on to the cow's tail while someone whips it into a frenzy."

"Poor cow! That's so cruel!"

She looked at him, amazed. "The person in the greased shoes gets trampled to death if they can't hold on. Why would you care about the cow?"

"Because it's done nothing wrong! Why should it be whipped?"

"Does it matter?"

"Yes, it does!" Joe could feel heat flooding into his cheeks. This was a losing battle with Lucy. He'd had these sorts of arguments with her before. But she would never see things his way because she was from such a different world. "So if the person gets trampled," he said, "it's supposed to show they were guilty, is it?"

"That's right. The gods help and protect the

innocent. Come on, we need to go and collect some heather."

Joe picked up his basket and followed her out of the copse and back to the track. He was glad to drop the subject, though less happy to be out in the wind again.

"What's the heather for?" he asked.

Lucy clicked her tongue. "You got all superior with me earlier on, when I didn't know what you were talking about, but you're still asking the daftest things! The heather is for the floor at home."

"Oh yes, of course." Joe tried to remember exactly what the house had been like. "There were grasses down when I was with you before, weren't there."

"Rushes," Lucy corrected him.

"Right." He shifted the basket to his other arm as they walked. It was starting to get heavy with the firewood. "Anyway, going back to Thorbiorn's chickens," he said, "if Peder didn't steal them, then who did?"

"That's a good question." Lucy was thoughtful. "We assumed it was some other boy who looked a bit like Peder, perhaps come into Jorvik from the countryside. We thought Thorbiorn had just made a mistake. But now I'm wondering ..."

"Was it actually Thorbiorn himself?" Joe finished her sentence for her.

"Exactly! Though I can't see why he would steal

his own chickens."

They both thought about this. "Perhaps he thought he'd make a bit of money by selling them," Joe said, "and try to cause trouble for your family at the same time."

Lucy's brows were drawn together. "It could be that, couldn't it? He would have had to sell them outside Jorvik, so that he wasn't recognised. But that's easy enough. And he was very quick to blame Peder." She stopped and wriggled the straps of the basket off her shoulders. "This heather will do." She bent down and began to cut short stems with her knife from the wiry plants around their feet.

Joe watched, holding his cloak close around him.

"Aren't you going to help me, then?"

"I don't have a knife."

She looked up. "We should do something about that. Snap the stems for now, and we'll ask my father when we get home."

Joe stooped down and did as she said. "He's home then, is he? Your father?"

"Of course!" Lucy glanced up. "He's been home months. We're well past mid-winter now. That's why I was so surprised to see you, after such a long time."

"And your brother? Did he come home safely?"

"Yes, thankfully. In fact, he'll be going again quite soon. But my mother's sacrifices to Odin worked once, so hopefully they'll work next time."

"What do you mean?"

"She made offerings of food every day so that Odin didn't take Mattheus to Valhalla." Lucy straightened up and pushed the bundles of heather into her basket in between the sticks.

Joe could feel her eyes on him. He tried to keep his face blank. But clearly it was too blank, because she said, "You don't have any idea what I'm talking about, do you?"

"Sorry," he mumbled. He avoided looking at her, breaking off the stems of heather until his hands were full and he had to stop and put it in his basket.

Lucy's eyes were still fixed on him, and one eyebrow was raised. "Would you like me to explain?"

"Yes, please," he said meekly.

"So, we live here on earth," she said, with exaggerated patience, "beneath a sky which is held up by four dwarves."

Joe burst out laughing. "Four dwarves! That's brilliant!"

She glared at him.

"You don't seriously believe that?" He grinned. "You'll be telling me next that the earth is flat!"

"That's because it is!" she said sharply. "Do you want me to tell you or not?"

Joe stifled his laughter. "Please go on," he said, as solemnly as he could.

"Thank you. Now, above the earth floats a place called Asgard where the gods live."

"You have more than one god?"

She glared at him again. "There are lots."

Joe bowed his head. "I see."

"The ruler of the Gods is Odin, the God of War and Death. He has a hall in Asgard called Valhalla. It's where warriors go when they die nobly, fighting to the death in battle. In Asgard, they're fed on pork and mead."

"Is that supposed to be a good thing?"

She tutted. "Of course it is! We're lucky if we eat meat twice in a week, never mind every day. And we only drink mead on special occasions. Besides, anyone would prefer to end up in Valhalla than Niflheim, which is where the rest of us will go when we die."

"Niflheim? That doesn't sound very nice."

"It isn't. It's the icy, dark afterworld, ruled over by Hel, goddess of the dead."

For a minute or two, they continued collecting heather without speaking.

Then Joe said, "If Valhalla is supposed to be a better place to end up than Niflheim, why was your mother asking Odin not to take Mattheus there?"

"Because he's too young to die just yet."

"What about your father then? She wanted him to come back alive from his last raid, but that must mean that he won't get another chance to get to Valhalla now. When's he ever going to fight in another battle?"

Lucy didn't answer right away. Joe wondered if he had somehow offended her with his question. After a while, she said, "I'd never thought about that. Maybe she wants him to be with her in the afterlife. Or maybe she doesn't believe in any of this anyway. In Ireland, when she was growing up, they had other ideas about what happens when you die. I don't really know what it was about - my father didn't want us to learn it. It's called Christeny or something like that."

"Do you mean Christianity?"

"Yes, that's it. You've heard of it then?"

Joe laughed. "You could say that!"

"Oh." She looked nonplussed. "Well last year," she went on, "the King of Jorvik agreed to do it, when he got married."

"Become a Christian, you mean?"

"That's right. For a while after that, my mother tried to get my father to agree to it as well. But then the King sent his new queen away and said he was giving it up. After that, my father got cross whenever my mother mentioned it. He just kept saying, 'If our way is good enough for the King, it's good enough for me.' "

She straightened up and stuffed the last of her heather into her basket. "We'll fill yours to the top, and then we need to be getting back."

"Aren't we staying out all day today?" Joe asked.

"No. Peder's taken the dogs to go hunting and there's nothing much else to bring back from out here.

There are no berries or nuts at this time of year. In any case, we usually do eat a bit of something in the middle of the day when it's this cold, to keep us going. Besides, it's bath day today."

"Is that a special occasion here?"

She laughed. "No! It's this day every week."

"Oh." Joe thought of the baths at Fishbourne. That had been one of the best afternoons there, apart from jumping into the plunge pool and nearly passing out. But he couldn't imagine the Viking bath experience would be quite so luxurious. Things were so much more primitive here in every way than they had been in Roman times. "I go with Peder, do I?" he asked.

"And my father and Mattheus."

"Will they be okay about having me around? What will your mother say about me turning up again after all this time?"

Lucy pushed a bundle of heather down in between the sticks in Joe's basket. "We'll tell them about Thorbiorn, that he threatened you."

"And that I disappeared?"

"Perhaps not that bit. We could say that he made you leave Jorvik, and you've only just dared come back."

"Will that be alright, do you think?"

"Should be, and in any case, I think they ought to know that you really did find Thorbiorn in our yard, even though he decided not to steal the chickens after all. Come on." She hoisted her basket on to her back. "Let's go."

A freezing drizzle was falling as they set off along the track back towards the city. Joe looked out across the bleak countryside to either side. There were very few trees and no bushes, and the wind was sweeping rain towards them like a curtain. He shivered inside his cloak. If only he had a hat or a hood like Lucy's. His hands were numb with cold too. He didn't know whether Vikings ever wore gloves. They had wool of course, but he hadn't seen anyone knitting last time he was here. In any case, from what he could remember from the books at school, the Viking people were so tough they probably didn't need them. He put his head down and trudged on.

After a while, he noticed Lucy humming under her breath.

"Don't tell me you're enjoying this!" he said.

"Of course not! But there's no point in thinking about how grim it is, is there? Better to hum a tune to pass the time."

Joe stomped on in silence. All the songs he knew at home had vanished from his head, as though washed away by the time slip. In any case, just right now he wasn't in the mood for pretending that things were better than they were. If he'd stayed in his own world, he'd be on a train now, sitting in the warm, dry carriage with a book to read and a bar of chocolate.

All of a sudden, he felt a stab of worry. The train

doors had opened at exactly the moment he was pulled out of his own world. Was there really no time at all passing at home while he was here? Even if it was just a few seconds, the doors might have closed again, and the train gone, leaving him on York station. He gulped. Dad wouldn't let that happen though, would he? As long as his body was still there, even if it seemed like he was asleep, Dad would have bundled him on to the train, surely. But what if he'd disappeared? There had never been a true test of what actually happened back at home when he slipped into Lucy's time.

"Nearly there," Lucy said.

Joe looked up. He'd been staring down at the track as he walked, trying to tell himself that there was no point worrying at the moment, since he couldn't do anything about it. Now, the walls of the city loomed up just ahead of them.

"By the way," he said, "do you still have my St. Christopher?"

"The pendant, you mean? Yes, of course. I'm wearing it now." Her hand went up to her neck.

"When I arrived here this morning, just before you came out to milk the goat, had you touched it or anything?"

"I hide it at night rather than wear it," she said, "and put it on when nobody's looking. So yes, I'd just touched it."

"And did you think of me?"

She looked across at him shyly. "I always think of you when I put it on. Why?"

"I think you called me here. Or rather we did it together, by me thinking of you at the same moment."

She looked surprised. "You were thinking of me?"

"Of course! I often think of you when I'm at home."

A flush of pink came into her pale cheeks. Joe felt his own cheeks colour as well. He didn't say anything else.

They hurried in through the gates in the city wall, keeping their heads down against the rain which was falling heavily now. This time, Joe thought he recognised the way.

At the end of their street, Lucy paused. "Ready to meet my father, then?" she asked.

Joe nodded. "At least, I'm as ready as I'm going to be!" He grinned.

She smiled back. "Right then. Let's go."

8

The man sitting at the lathe in the workshop had shoulder-length, blond hair and a neatly trimmed beard. Behind him, kneeling on the ground, sawing a piece of wood into strips, was a youth of sixteen or seventeen with similarly long hair.

"Hello!" Lucy called, as they approached.

Both men looked up. "You caught it out there in the rain!" Her father grinned. "I thought you might have come back sooner."

Lucy stood in the open front of the workshop. "Father, Mattheus, this is Joe." She beckoned to Joe to come forward. "He stayed with us overnight while you were both away."

Lucy's father nodded in greeting. "I'm Lokki."

Joe gave a little bow.

Mattheus was looking curiously at him. Joe realised he'd been narrowing his eyes, trying to imagine the two men with short black hair. They probably were the same people they'd been in Roman times, Lucy's father Lucullus, and her eldest brother

Marius, though with so much blond hair it was more difficult to be certain than it had been with the girls. He blinked and nodded in greeting.

"Aren't you the one that disappeared into the night without a word?" Mattheus said.

Before Joe could reply, Lucy answered for him. "That's right. It turns out Thorbiorn frightened him off."

"Thorbiorn?" Lokki cocked his head to one side. "That boy's up to some tricks these days. It'll be a good thing when he's old enough to go off raiding. What happened?"

Joe glanced at Lucy.

"Tell them," she said.

"Thorbiorn was out in the yard when I went out with the moss," Joe said. "He was about to steal your chickens. I tried to stop him, but he pulled out his knife and said I should disappear. So I did." He suppressed a smile at his own little joke. "Perhaps I was stupid to be scared," he went on. "But I really thought he might kill me."

"He wouldn't have done that." Lokki shook his head. "But he's a good few years older than you and a lot bigger. I'm not surprised you were frightened. Still, you obviously did stop him, because we still have the same chickens now. So we're in your debt for that." He scratched his beard thoughtfully. "Interesting," he said, more to himself than to anyone else. And then, "Mattheus and I are just finishing up here. By the time you've swept out the house and put that heather down, we'll be in."

Joe followed Lucy into the living area of the house. After being outside, it felt nice and warm, though it was very dark, just as before. This time, however, as well as the fire, there were two lamps made with pieces of burning reed, each one casting a small pool of light around it. Beside one stood Sorcha, helping Aine with her weaving at the loom. Lucy's mother sat beside the other lamp, mending something.

She looked up as they entered. "Hello, Luiseach. Who's that with you?" She squinted in the half-light. "It's not the boy, Joe, is it?"

"Yes, he's back!" Lucy squeezed Joe's arm. "Tell her what happened, Joe. Tell her why you left."

So Joe explained, just as he had done to Lucy's father.

Aileen listened and tutted. "Thorbiorn's getting out of control," she said. "Well, Joe, you're welcome to stay with us again, though we're a bit more cosy here, now that my husband and son are home."

"Thank you." He smiled. It was good to be among people who accepted him so easily. "Lokki said we should sweep the floor. Shall we do it now?"

"What? And spread all that damp heather over it?" Aileen laughed. "It'll stay wet till it rots! He's a good cooper and a great warrior, but he doesn't know much about housekeeping!" She pointed to a basket hanging on the wall near the fire. "Put the heather in there, so that it can dry out. We'll leave the rushes down until later."

"Is Peder not back yet?" asked Lucy.

"No, but he should be soon. Take off your wet cloaks and hang them up, then sort out your baskets. If there's time after that before the others come in, you can start combing that wool."

Joe shadowed Lucy, hanging his cloak beside hers, and putting all of their heather in the basket. He was hoping that Peder and the others would come in and save him from having to work out what to do with the wool. But there was still no sign of them by the time he and Lucy had stacked their firewood along the wall of the house. Lucy dragged the wool basket into the light of the fire and fetched a second, empty one.

"We're going to pick it over to begin with," she muttered. "We'll put it in this basket as we do it, and then I'll start combing."

Joe nodded, grateful that she'd guessed he wouldn't know what to do. He copied her, taking a bundle of fleece and picking out all the bits of mud, grass and dried sheep poo.

"You squash anything that's alive," Lucy whispered, pouncing on some kind of insect about to spring off the wool. She crushed it with her thumb nail, flicked it into the fire, and carried on. The rest of what she picked out, she threw down on the floor beside her.

Presently, there was the sound of voices at the

door. Aileen put her mending aside and stood up. Just like last time, she began to fill wooden bowls with stew from the pot hanging over the fire. On the table was a plate of dark brown flatbreads. Sorcha left the loom and set out cups and spoons, and the same tall flagon of barley beer. Joe tried to prepare himself mentally for another meal ordeal.

Lucy's father entered the room first, followed by Mattheus and Peder. They took off their cloaks, while the dogs snuffled around beneath the table. Suddenly, the animals noticed Joe. Just like before, the fur stood up on their backs and they began to growl.

"What's the matter with you, stupid beasts?" Mattheus nudged one of them with his foot. It didn't move a muscle.

Joe flinched, waiting for the dogs to leap at him.

"It's Joe," Lucy said. "For some reason, they're scared of him." She stood up, putting herself between them and Joe. "Go on with you, now!" she commanded. "Leave him alone and go and lie down." She pointed to a corner of the room. "Now!"

After a moment, the dogs turned and slunk off.

"Well, well," Lokki said. "I've never seen them behave like that! You clearly have mysterious powers, Joe! They think we need protecting from you!"

Joe laughed uncertainly.

But Lokki seemed to be joking. He came to stand in front of the fire and rubbed his hands together. "No sign of spring yet," he remarked. "The rain's turning to sleet. If we're in for another freeze, we should get the skates out again."

Joe looked up, surprised. He'd never imagined people as far back as the Vikings ice-skating.

"Peder's brought back some grayling," Mattheus said. "Just as well, since we must be nearly out of pork now."

"That pig's done us well." Aileen rapped the ladle on the edge of the pot. "It's fed us three months, and we're not through it yet."

Joe remembered the empty pig pen outside. "Will you get another one?" he asked.

"In the spring, yes. Then we'll fatten him up over the summer and he'll feed us next winter."

They took it in turns to rinse their hands in the water bowl, and then sat down to eat. Joe was grateful to find the stew much tastier this time. Amongst the vegetables were small pieces of meat, tasting strongly of salt, which flavoured the rest of the food. The flatbreads however were heavy, and although his one crumbled as he broke it, he had to chew and chew before he could swallow it. There was grit in it too which ground between his teeth like sand in a beach picnic.

"How are we doing for beans?" Lokki asked. "We must be getting through them, now that there's no more rye to be had."

"We are." Aileen dipped her bread in her soup. "I'm going to have to use the rest of them for flour.

There aren't many peas either. We've eaten nearly everything we dried last year. I just hope the spring crops come through early."

"Can we ask cousin Finwith to help?" Peder asked.

Lokki shook his head. "We've already had the exchange for the horse."

"What horse?" Joe asked. He peered through the gloom towards the end of the room where the dogs were lying.

"Not here!" Lucy laughed. "Cousin Finwith keeps our horse with his own animal. He has a farmstead a few miles outside Jorvik."

"That's nice of him."

She shrugged. "There's plenty of room. And there's plenty of work for two horses, at some times of the year at least. We get some of his harvest in exchange. It's a good arrangement for everyone."

Lokki picked up his bowl and tipped the last of his stew into his mouth, wiping round afterwards with the end of his bread. Then he drained his cup of beer and stood up. It hadn't been a very big meal for such a large man, Joe thought, but he didn't seem to expect anything else.

"Come on then, boys. Hurry up and finish. We need to get down to the baths. Where's your grooming set, Mattheus?"

Lucy's eldest brother stuffed his bread into his mouth and washed it down with beer. "I'll just get it," he said, still chewing.

"I don't have a grooming set," Joe whispered to Lucy.

"Don't worry." She smiled. "Nor does Peder, and nor do Aine and I. You only get one at fourteen. Before that, you share other people's."

"What is it anyway?"

"Tweezers, nail cleaners, comb, ear scoop."

"Ear scoop?"

"Yes, for getting the wax out of your ears!"

Joe grimaced.

"Why are you looking like that? It's useful stuff, earwax, especially for spinning wool."

"Yuck!"

Her eyes danced with laughter at his disgust.

"Come on then!" Lokki had picked up his cloak and hat and was at the door again. "Time to go. You're coming with us, Joe?"

Joe nodded, his mouth still full of bread. He grabbed his own cloak from the peg and followed Mattheus and Peder out of the house.

The bath house was a few minutes walk from Coppergate, a large chalet-like building with wooden walls and a low thatched roof. From one end of the building rose a column of smoke, while a faint mist hovered over the thatch. A line of men and boys huddled outside in the sleet, talking and laughing together. Joe hugged his damp cloak around him and watched what was going on. He felt exposed, being out of the house without Lucy. She might not really understand how alien her world was to him, but she had more idea than her brothers or her father.

Every few minutes a small group of people came out of the chalet and the line moved forward. Soon, they were at the front. Joe wondered what would be inside the building. It wasn't large enough to have a pool of any size.

When the next group of people came out, he followed Lokki and the others in. It was warm inside and they were standing in a small changing area with smoking reed lamps on the walls. Beneath were wooden benches and pegs hung with clothes. Joe undressed, trying not to look as the others took off their undershorts. Even though he'd done this before at Fishbourne, he still felt self-conscious about being naked in front of other people.

Lokki opened a door to an inner chamber and hustled them all in, closing the door quickly behind them. The room was twice the width of the changing area, and similarly dark, but as hot as if they had stepped into a desert. Joe sat down beside Peder on a bench, grateful that the heat was dry rather than steamy.

There were twenty men and boys in the room in total, most of them sitting motionless on the benches down either side. Down at the far end was a fire, and above it, the hole in the roof where Joe had seen the smoke escaping. Around the fire were piles of large round stones. Now and then, someone poured a cup of water over them. There was a loud hiss, and the temperature seemed to rise sharply. Joe felt sweat break out all over his skin. He felt a wave of panic, just like in the caldarium at Fishbourne. He concentrated hard on keeping calm.

After a while, Lokki and Mattheus stood up and moved to the middle of the room. From an open box they each picked up a bundle of twigs which they beat against their skin systematically, beginning with their necks and shoulders, and working their way down to their feet. Joe watched, wondering whether it hurt.

When Lokki and Mattheus sat down again, Peder stood up. Joe got up too, and picked up one of the bundles. The twigs were thin and supple, and much less scratchy than he'd feared. Cautiously, he started to flick them against his skin. It didn't hurt. In fact, it felt quite pleasant, a bit like scratching an itch. He began to hit his arms and chest a little harder, copying Peder, though he was mystified by why they might be doing this. By the time he'd worked his way down to his ankles, his skin was tingling all over.

He sat down again beside Mattheus. He and Lokki had been combing their long hair, and offered their combs now to Joe and Peder. Joe took Lokki's. It was carved out of a single piece of bone, short, with long teeth on both sides, all of which were intact. He remembered the broken combs in the glass cases at the Viking Centre and grinned. Archaeologists would give anything to hold a perfect object like this in their hands!

They sat for a while longer in the hot darkness. Occasionally, men left through a door beside the one where they had entered, and others came in. Each man in turn beat himself with the birch twigs.

At length, Lokki stood up and opened the second door. It was much cooler in the small room on the other side. Lokki took a cloth from a peg and dipped it in a bucket of water. Mattheus and Peder did likewise, and after a moment's hesitation, so did Joe. Each of them rubbed their skin all over with the cloth before rinsing it in a second bucket and hanging it back on the peg.

None of them spoke as they dressed again in the changing area, but Joe found that he felt more relaxed than he had done since he arrived.

"Looks like we could be rolling in the snow after next week's bath," Mattheus said, as they emerged into the daylight. Joe looked up at the sky. The sleet had stopped, but the clouds were a heavy grey tinged with yellow. He pulled his cloak close, glad that there hadn't been snow on the ground to roll in today.

The queue of men and boys was longer than it had been when they arrived. Joe eyed them as he walked past. They were mostly tall and blond, with broad shoulders and hair that was somewhat unkempt compared to the men coming out of the baths. Some of them had a single ponytail, and some had two bunches or even plaits. He was just pondering the variety of styles, and the age at which they started to grow it long, when he saw a face he recognised. It was Thorbiorn.

Joe's footsteps faltered. The other boy had clearly spotted him the moment he'd stepped out of the bath house and was staring at him with open malice. Joe glanced towards Lokki and the others, but they were a few paces ahead. He looked back at Thorbiorn again. The older boy had not taken his eyes off him.

Instinctively, Joe shrank away. He hadn't done anything to harm Thorbiorn. But his disappearance from the yard that night must have rattled the older boy. Now, he was bound to guess that Joe would have told Lucy's family everything.

He hurried to catch up with Peder. All the way along the street, he was sure he could feel Thorbiorn's eyes boring into his back. Panic made his chest tight. He'd been hoping he wouldn't encounter Lucy's cousin again, at least not for a while. But he hadn't managed even one day.

He tried to pull himself together. The other boy had only looked at him, nothing more. There was no need to worry.

But he knew what Thorbiorn was capable of. He'd been quick to draw his knife last time, and there was no getting away from what he'd been like in Lucy's previous world, as Tiberius. Joe shuddered. At the very least, he knew he would be included now in Thorbiorn's hatred of Lucy's family. Worse, it was possible that he himself had become the focus of that hatred.

He walked beside Peder, silent and anxious, wondering what to do. He would talk to Lucy when he got back, he decided. Perhaps she would have an idea.

9

Lucy wasn't at home when they let themselves into the house. Nor were Aileen, Sorcha or Aine.

Seeing Joe looking around for them, Peder said, "They've gone to the women's baths." He drew up a stool beside the wool baskets, fetched a teasel, and began to comb the fleece that Joe and Lucy had picked over.

Mattheus lit both reed lamps and went to the loom to continue the weaving that Aine had been working on. Lokki poured beer into the cups which were still on the table. "Have a drink, Joe," he said, holding one out to him. "It's a good idea after the baths."

Joe took the cup and pulled up a stool opposite Peder. "Do you work all day, every day?" he asked.

"No," Peder said. "There's a bit of time most days to play outside, or else we do something together when the important jobs are done."

"But not now?"

"Now? I don't know about you, but I'm not

really in the mood for playing football or anything like that."

"No, I suppose not." Joe took a bundle of fleece from the basket and began picking it over, glad that there was something he knew how to do.

Lokki built up the fire, and then disappeared out of the back door to the yard.

"So if you're indoors, you do something useful?" Joe asked.

"Not always. But you may as well when half the family is out." Peder shrugged. "Clapping and singing games don't work very well when there are only two of you. Dice is better with more people too. We could play hnefatafl, I suppose, but that would be better outside where you can see the board and the pieces properly. I'd say it's a bit cold for that."

Joe thought about this. At home, if he was indoors, he would read a book or watch television, or he might play with his technic Lego or do something on the computer. But they didn't have any of those things to do here. They didn't even have paper and pencils for drawing.

For some time, the three boys worked in silence. Joe guessed that Lucy's brothers probably felt the same sense of calm that he'd felt as they left the baths. He, on the other hand, was still worrying about Thorbiorn, and whether Thorbiorn would set out to hurt him deliberately. He wished Lucy would come back.

Presently, they heard voices outside the house. Lucy pushed open the door, followed by her mother and sisters. "Guess what?" she cried. Joe blinked, startled by how loud her voice sounded in the quietness of the room. "There's a storyteller arrived in Jorvik!" Lucy danced around the table. "We saw Inga at the baths. She's invited us over this evening to hear him!"

Mattheus stopped weaving. "That's great!"

"Fantastic!" Peder jumped to his feet.

Joe looked at Sorcha and Aine. Their faces were also bright with delight. It was clearly an important event. He smiled and nodded, trying to pretend he shared their excitement.

"What's all this?" Lokki asked, coming in from the yard.

"A storyteller! At Inga's this evening!"

"Marvellous! We've got a jar of mead we can take. It's about time there was another gathering. There's been nothing since the horse fighting two moons ago."

"Horses? Fighting?" Joe muttered to Peder.

Lucy's brother nodded. "Not our horse. Or other working horses. They're specially bred stallions. They often fight to the death! It's really exciting!"

"Is it?" Joe couldn't keep the doubt out of his voice. The idea of such gentle animals being made to fight was somehow rather nasty.

"Well, I prefer storytelling," Lucy said, pulling

up a stool beside Joe. "They tell such amazing tales of battles and voyages!"

"Tall tales, more like!" Mattheus said from the loom. "I've never heard a story of a voyage that didn't include a sea monster, but we didn't see a single one in all the time we were away!"

"Maybe you just weren't in the right place!" Lucy said.

"Maybe. Perhaps they'd gone south to warmer waters!" Mattheus laughed.

The mood in the house was jolly for the rest of the afternoon. Each member of the family took it in turns to come and sit on a low stool at Aileen's feet, while she combed carefully through their hair.

"Is she looking for something?" Joe whispered to Lucy.

"Yes, of course! Nits, ticks and fleas."

"Oh no!"

"Well at least if you look, you can get rid of them! We take care of ourselves here, unlike the southerners. They're hopping with life, and they hardly ever wash. It's disgusting!" She shuddered.

When Aileen had finished, Lokki took her place and combed through her hair, keeping up a patter of conversation, gossip and jokes all the while. In the meantime, everyone else worked at the task they had chosen, joining in with the banter or keeping quiet, as they wished. Joe was surprised to feel real satisfaction at being part of all this. He wondered idly how Sam would cope. Not very well, he thought, especially with being parted from his phone.

They ate supper early, the same stew and bread as at lunchtime, and then began to get ready to go out. Joe watched from the fireside as Aileen lifted some planks which lay across the floor at the far end of the room. Beneath was a deep, rectangular hole, almost completely filled by a chest. She lifted the lid and brought out for each person a set of clothes made from more brightly coloured fabric than their day-to-day clothes. From a box inside the chest came a selection of ornamental brooches, belts, and clothes pins, and then a tiny pot with a lid and a thin piece of bone with a blunt end. She opened the pot, dipped the bone into it, and then drew dark lines carefully around her eyes. Then she turned to Sorcha, Lokki, and Mattheus and did the same. Joe watched, fascinated. He'd never seen men wearing eye-liner before.

While everyone else was changing their clothes, Aileen came over to him. "Do you have anything else to wear, Joe?" she asked quietly.

He shook his head.

"Would you like to borrow something? I have some clothes which are too small for Peder now."

"Are you sure? What if I spill something? I wouldn't want to spoil them."

Aileen smiled wistfully. "It doesn't matter if you do. I don't have another little boy who will wear them."

Joe frowned. In her other life at Fishbourne, Lucy had had a younger brother who'd died. Perhaps the same child was missing from this family. He hadn't thought to ask Lucy about it.

He took the clothes and put them on. They weren't very different in style to the clothes he'd taken off, but the fabric was finer and the colours more vivid. He felt a good deal smarter in them.

"Are we ready?" Lokki asked at last. "Each of you youngsters please bring a stool or a sheepskin to sit on. I have the mead and the drinking horn. Your mother has food." He looked around at them all. "What a fine family!" he beamed. "Come on then! Let's go!"

Joe was the last person out of the house. "Should I lock the door or something?" he asked.

"No." Aileen swung the cord which hung down from her belt, like the one Lucy had to carry her knife. A pair of heavy iron keys clinked. "The few valuable things we have are locked away. Just make sure it's shut so the dogs don't wander off."

Joe gave the door an extra tug, just to be sure, and then followed the rest of the family through the cold, dark streets. The sky had cleared, and as he walked, he looked up at the moon and stars above. It was strange to think that it was the same moon, the same stars which would shine on him at home, a thousand years from now.

Suddenly, in the middle of all the excitement, he

felt a surge of homesickness. If only he could go back, just for half an hour, or for tea maybe, and then come back here and carry on. He felt like he hadn't seen Dad in ages, though it was only this morning, even in Lucy's time. And he hadn't seen Mum in a week.

But of course, it wasn't possible. He swallowed, and clenched his teeth until the prickling behind his eyes and nose had stopped.

The house they came to looked exactly the same to Joe as Lucy's house, long and narrow with a workshop at the front.

"Inga's husband is a silversmith," Lucy said in Joe's ear. "Look how much nicer their place is."

Joe looked, but couldn't see what she meant. "In what way?"

"That stuff plastered over the outside of the walls makes it warmer."

"It makes it smellier too! What is it?"

"Animal dung. But it only smells because it was done recently. Soon, you won't notice it. And there are windows in it too!"

"Windows?" He peered through the darkness. "Do you mean that there?" He pointed to a tiny square above the door whose texture was different to the rest of the walls.

"That's right!" Lucy was full of awe. "You're probably thinking it must let the cold in, but it's covered over with pig's bladder, so there's no draught!"

Joe pressed his lips together to keep himself from laughing. "Does it let in any light? Or is it just for show?"

Lucy didn't notice his sarcasm. "Of course it lets light in! And they have them in every wall!"

"Goodness!" Joe did his best to sound impressed, since that was clearly what Lucy expected.

"It's a pity we're here after nightfall. You should see what it's like in the day!"

They followed the rest of the family inside.

Behind the workshop was a single large room, just as in Lucy's house. The same kind of reed lamps had been mounted on the walls as in the bath house, but they guttered and smoked, so it was still far from bright. It was also incredibly hot and crowded.

"Come in! Come in!" roared a bear of a man with fiery red hair and beard. "The more the merrier! We'll find space for everyone somewhere!"

They edged into the room, climbing round and over people already seated on stools or on the floor. The air buzzed with chatter. Lucy found a space, and spread her sheepskin down on the ground, and then her cloak on top of it. Joe laid his cloak down on top of hers, and squeezed in beside her, passing back the stool he'd brought for Aileen to use. More and more people arrived, until he guessed there were probably a hundred or more crammed in shoulder to shoulder, some almost on top of each other.

When the last remaining inch of space had been

filled, a man who had been standing at the front picked his way across to a tall stool beside the fire. Immediately, the room was quiet. He sat down and began to speak, his voice rising and falling in a singsong rhythm.

Joe listened, bewildered. The story was in rhyme, and peopled with characters that everyone else seemed to know. An old man sitting on the edge of the room even appeared to know the words, because his lips moved in time with the storyteller's. The language was much more flowery than Joe was used to, and it took him some time to realise that 'wound dew' meant 'blood' and the 'whale's road' was the sea. Gradually, however, he picked up the gist of the tale, about giants, and goblins, and gods, and by the end, he was gripped.

When the story had finished, there was a brief pause whilst some of the listeners shuffled round. And then the second story began, of a ship crossing the sea to a new country, of storms and fierce winds, and a monster curled around an island, keeping the people who lived there prisoners. At the end of this tale, cups of barley beer were passed round to the children, while the adults passed drinking horns like Lokki's to one another, lifting them to their lips to drink the mead. Trays of food were handed round, with bread and cheese, and dried fruit. Nobody took very much, Joe noticed. He helped himself to some dried apple and sipped his beer. Perhaps he was getting used to it at last, because it didn't taste as bad as when he'd first been given it.

By the end of the third story, he was feeling pleasantly sleepy. The younger children had fallen asleep already, their heads on their mothers' laps. Joe drew up his knees and rested his chin on his arms. The storyteller had changed tack now, and was narrating a saga for the adults, of love and lust, deception, betrayal and revenge. Joe soon found that he'd lost track of who was who. People seemed to keep being killed, rather like the feud that Lucy had told him about. He closed his eyes and let his mind drift, imagining being at home again, with Mum and Sam. Only Thorbiorn was somehow there too, prancing about, and then drawing his knife the moment Mum looked away.

It seemed only a few minutes later that Joe felt himself shaken awake. He opened his eyes and looked around in panic. But Thorbiorn was nowhere to be seen.

"Come on, sleepy heads!" Mattheus said. "It's time to go home."

Joe and Lucy stumbled to their feet and pulled their cloaks around them. Mattheus picked up the sheepskin, and they let themselves be carried by the tide of people out of the house on to the moonlit street.

"Goodnight! Goodnight!" voices shouted all around them.

Joe rubbed his eyes, glad to have been woken

from the dream, but still aching to sleep again. Jorvik was a blur, dark and shadowy, and freezing cold. *I must tell Lucy about Thorbiorn,* he murmured to himself as he trailed along behind Mattheus. *I must tell Lucy about Thorbiorn.*

Back at the house, however, he rolled into bed beside Peder and was asleep in moments.

He was woken early the following morning by frantic whispering. It was still dark in the room. He lay for a while watching the mist of his breath rise from his mouth, trying to work out what was going on.

"They can't be!" hissed Aileen.

"They definitely are," replied Lokki.

"Did you check them last night?"

"Of course not! After all that mead? I didn't think of anything except my bed!"

"So they were like this then?"

"Must have been. I assumed they were asleep."

"They don't look very asleep!"

"Don't blame me, woman!" Lokki's voice rose. "You didn't notice either!"

Further down the room, Mattheus stirred. "What's the matter?" he asked blearily.

There was a pause.

"It's the dogs," his father answered at last.

Joe heard Aileen stifle a sob.

"Someone came in while we were out last night. They've been poisoned."

10

"Poisoned? No!" Lucy cried.

Joe sat up and pulled on his tunic. Lucy had jumped out of bed. She must have been lying there listening just like him.

"I'm afraid so."

"But who would do such a terrible thing?"

"Was anything taken?" Mattheus asked.

Aileen carried her reed lamp down to the end of the room. She lifted some planks from the floor beside the ones she had moved the day before. Beneath them was an even larger hole, and in it, an enormous chest.

She knelt down. "It doesn't look like anyone's touched it." She took one of the keys from the end of the cord that hung from her belt and fitted it into the lock. "It's alright. Everything's still in here."

"Including the horn?" Lokki asked.

"Yes."

"Well, that's the most important thing!"

"But who would be so cruel?" Lucy cried again, moving towards where the dogs were lying.

Her father caught her in his arms. "Don't touch them, Luiseach! They feel different, now they're dead. You won't like it." He stroked her hair while she sobbed into his chest. "I have an idea who it might have been." His face was grim in the half-light. "But whether we'll be able to prove it is another question."

Mattheus had pulled on his clothes. "I'll go and start digging a grave."

"I'll help you." Lokki stood Lucy back on her feet and took two spades down from hooks. "Luiseach, Joe, wake the others and then go and fetch some water so we can start our day." He followed Mattheus out into the yard.

Joe roused Peder and then put on the rest of his clothes. At the door, Aileen gave him and Lucy two wooden buckets each. She opened the door for them and glanced up and down the street, as though the intruder might still be somewhere nearby. But there was no-one about.

It was even colder this morning as they set off across town together. Joe shivered. A few flakes of snow gathered in doorways, and the ground was frozen hard. Lucy had stopped crying, but she didn't speak.

"Where do we get the water?" Joe asked.

"The river," she said. "Mother thinks it's cleaner. Anyway, there'll be a queue at the well on this side of town, unless it's frozen over."

They walked on in silence again. Gradually, other people were emerging from their houses, many of them also carrying buckets.

After a bit, Joe said, "The horn your father mentioned, is that supposed to be the unicorn's horn?"

"Sssh!" Lucy's eyes flared and she looked around quickly to see if he'd been overheard. "How did you know we had one?"

"You told me, remember, when I first arrived."

"Not so loud!" she whispered.

"Why not?" Joe dropped his voice. "You know it isn't really from a unicorn. They don't exist!"

"Yes, it is! Mattheus told me. It has magical powers! That's why my father wanted to be sure it hadn't been taken."

"What kind of powers?" Joe tried unsuccessfully to keep the sarcasm out of his voice.

But Lucy ignored his tone. "Healing powers, for one thing. You can grind it up to use in spells. And it can protect you, too."

Joe grinned. "So where did Mattheus tell you it had come from?"

Lucy glared at him. "It belonged to my grandfather. He brought it back with him from one of his voyages far away. When he was killed, he left it to my father's brother, who in turn left it to my father when *he* died."

"Your grandfather was killed in the feud, wasn't he? How did your uncle die?"

"In battle."

"But if the unicorn's horn is supposed to heal

and protect, surely it should have saved him!"

Joe watched with satisfaction while Lucy struggled to think of an answer.

"He wouldn't have had it with him, of course!" she said, after a few moments, sticking out her chin. "And anyway, dying in battle is a good thing, like I was telling you yesterday."

"Hang on." Joe frowned. "Is this the same brother that killed Thorbiorn's father?"

Lucy nodded. "That's another reason why Thorbiorn hates our family. His father will have gone to Niflheim after my uncle killed him. But my uncle himself died a glorious death, so he's gone to Valhalla."

"Is that really right? Don't you believe in some kind of punishment after death if someone murders someone else?"

"It was Thorbiorn's family that started the feud," Lucy said.

Joe shook his head. "All the same ..."

"Anyway," Lucy said firmly, "the horn was given to my father."

"So why is it such a secret?"

She glanced around again, and then whispered, "Because it's incredibly valuable, of course! People pay a fortune for a few grains of its magical dust."

"Why don't you sell it, then? Just think, you could be rich! You could have a big house and servants, and eat meat every day!"

Lucy was shocked. "We can't do that! There

were words that came with it. Mattheus told me. I don't know where from, perhaps from the unicorn itself." She recited solemnly:

"*Be sure of the horn to take good care,*

Your house shall else be cursed! Beware!"

"But that's nonsense!" Joe spluttered with laughter. "The rhyme only just makes sense, and even if there *was* such a thing as a unicorn - which there isn't - it couldn't talk, never mind put a curse on you! Mattheus has been pulling your leg!"

Lucy hunched her shoulders. He could see she was offended, but he couldn't let it go. "Can't you see?" he persisted. "If it did what you say, it would have kept your household safe. But what about your little brother who died?"

She stopped in her tracks. "How do you know about Frethi?" she asked, alarmed. "I've never told you about him! We don't talk about him. It upsets my mother."

"I just know," Joe said. "Like I was trying to tell you before, I knew you in a different time. Your little brother's name was Flavius then."

Lucy took a step sideways away from him and walked on again, keeping a wide gap between them. "You scare me sometimes," she muttered. "Anyway, you're wrong!" She pulled her cloak tighter around her. "It does work! All of us were ill when we were small. Aine was really, really ill just after Frethi. But he was the only one who died."

"How is that supposed to be good?"

She glared at him again. "Every other family I know has lost at least two babies or children, sometimes three or even more!"

Joe said nothing. He tried to imagine what it might be like, to have several brothers or sisters who'd died. But it was hard enough to imagine being one of five or six children in the first place.

They reached the river, and knelt down on the bank to fill the buckets. The force of the water nearly dragged Joe in. He grabbed a tussock of frosty grass and hung on to it while he hauled the first bucket out. It was really heavy. He filled the second bucket. As they started for home again, icy water slopped over his feet.

"These weigh a ton!" he said, stopping after a few steps to dry his hands on his cloak and get a better grip. "My arms are going to be like a gorilla's by the time we get back."

Lucy looked at him scornfully, but didn't answer. Of course, he realised, she wouldn't know what a gorilla was. Nonetheless, he couldn't help noticing that she had no trouble carrying her buckets, even though they were as large and as full as his own, and she herself wasn't any bigger than him. He felt vaguely annoyed.

Neither of them spoke as they walked back. In the house, the fire was roaring again. Aileen took the buckets and poured water from the first of them into the porridge pot which hung over the fire. Beside the hearth was a large space on the floor where the dogs had been. Joe couldn't help feeling a little bit relieved, though he knew better than to show it.

Lucy's mouth was set in a stubborn line. She picked up a spindle and began to spin the wool Peder had combed the previous afternoon.

"What will you do about the dogs?" Joe asked Aileen, pulling up a stool beside Aine to carry on picking over the fleece.

Lucy's mother stirred the porridge. "What do you mean, 'do'?"

"Will you report it? If someone's been into your house and killed your animals, shouldn't somebody do something about it?"

She shrugged. "Lokki's gone to tell one of the town elders, and Mattheus and Sorcha are asking up and down the street if anyone saw anything. Apart from that, there's not much we can do."

"But I thought Lokki knew who'd done it," Joe said.

Aileen shook her head. "He thinks it might have been Thorbiorn. But unless anyone actually saw him come into our house, we can't be certain."

A niggling worry crept into Joe's mind. For a long time, he looked into the fire.

Then he said, "Do you think it might have something to do with me being here?"

Aileen frowned. "How could it? You were with us last night for the storytelling. We know you didn't do it, even if the dogs were a bit funny about you."

"It's only that Thorbiorn saw me as I was leaving the baths yesterday, so he knows I'm back. The way he looked at me ..." Joe hesitated.

"What?"

"It just - well, it frightened me a bit," he mumbled.

Aileen smiled kindly. "That's Thorbiorn for you, I'm afraid. He likes to bully and frighten younger children. I don't suppose it was aimed particularly at you, except that you were with my sons. You see, he doesn't like our family."

"I know."

There was a pause.

Then Lucy said, "I wonder if you're right though, somehow."

He looked up at her. Her irritation with him seemed to have gone.

"You stopped him from stealing our chickens when you were here before. You might have scared him too. Perhaps he hopes we'll blame you for the dogs, as though you're the bringer of bad luck or something."

Joe nodded miserably. "I'm not, you know. Really."

Aileen put a hand on his shoulder. "Of course you're not!"

They worked on together in silence, Aine and Joe picking over the wool, Peder combing it and Lucy spinning. Aileen had rolled up her sleeves and started kneading bread dough.

After some time, Mattheus and Sorcha returned.

"Well? Did anyone see anything?"

They shook their heads. "Everyone was indoors," Sorcha said, "except for the people we saw at Inga's. They all came home the same time we did, which was too late."

"I'm going to go round there," growled Mattheus. "Somebody has to teach that boy a lesson!"

"You'll do no such thing!" Aileen said curtly. "Your father will deal with this as he thinks best."

"But if it *is* Thorbiorn, he'll do nothing! You know that! He feels so guilty that the boy has no father, he'll just let him get away with it! But Thorbiorn wants to provoke us. Don't you see? He won't stop until he does!"

The muscles in Aileen's neck were taut. "It's clear he wants to breathe new life into the feud," she said. "But we can't let him!"

"So we just turn a blind eye?" Mattheus' voice rose in outrage. "First he steals our fish, then he accuses Peder of theft, and now, the dogs! What next?"

At that moment, Lokki burst in. "What on earth is going on in here?" he demanded. "I could hear you from the street!"

"Mattheus wants to take matters into his own hands." Aileen pummelled the dough with her fists.

Lokki pulled out a stool and sat down. "Don't do

that, son," he said wearily. He rested his head in his hands. "The thing is, we don't know for sure that it *was* Thorbiorn. The dogs might have eaten something poisonous during the day, and we didn't notice. And even if it *was* him, you punishing him won't put an end to it." He looked up. "The elders say we should raise it at the next gathering. So let's forget about it for now."

Aileen nodded. "Why don't you make yourself useful, Mattheus?" she said. "Serve out the porridge."

They sat down in silence. Joe forced himself to eat his, but he couldn't shake off the feeling that all this was somehow connected to him.

After breakfast, Lokki and Mattheus opened up the workshop and Aileen sent the rest of them out for some fresh air. It was too cold to sit still, so they wandered through the town, not speaking much, at a loss for what to do. In one of the open spaces Joe had noticed before, they came to a market.

Lucy didn't seem very interested, and Aine, Peder and Sorcha had soon drifted away. But Joe wanted to have a closer look. "Do you mind?" he asked. "You look bored."

"It's not that." Lucy raised her eyes from her feet. "Normally, I like this kind of market. I'm just not in the mood today."

"If you want to go back, I'll be fine on my own," he said.

She half smiled. "Will you? You don't think you might get lost? Or land yourself in trouble again?"

"I might," he conceded.

"It's alright. You can look round for as long as you like. There isn't actually anything I want to do, so I may as well stay with you."

Together, they ambled through the stalls. The traders were haggling with their customers, exchanging things for snippets of silver, or for one of the baskets of squawking chickens and geese that seemed to be everywhere. But they weren't selling the kinds of things Joe would have expected, like fish or meat or eggs. These stalls were offering animal skins and jewellery; there were figures carved from what looked like ivory, and bowls made of stone. He gazed around wide-eyed. The most popular stalls were selling polished amber and glass beads, silver and bronze dishes with intricate patterns, and brightly coloured fabrics.

"That's silk, isn't it?" He pointed to some strips of material woven with gleaming red and gold thread. "And the spices, they must be from the Middle East! This is amazing! How on earth does it get here?"

Lucy shrugged. "The men sometimes trade when they're away, so they bring things back from further away than they can sail. We can't afford much of it though. The silk especially is incredibly expensive, even for a tiny piece."

"It really is amazing!" Joe said again, stopping in front of a stall selling shining swords and axes. "You'd never find a market like this where I come from! And yet, we think we have everything!"

At last, when he'd finally had enough, they walked on together towards the river.

On one of the bridges, they stopped and looked down at the water. Lucy was still very quiet.

"Is there really nothing that can be done about Thorbiorn?" Joe said. "It does seem wrong that he can get away with something as cruel as killing your animals."

She sighed. "You heard what my parents said. They'd be furious if any of us tried to get revenge in any obvious way. The only thing we could do would be -" She broke off.

"What?"

"Well ..." She paused. "There's a wise woman I've heard of. People get spells and curses from her."

"Really?" Joe made a big effort to swallow his disbelief.

"The problem is, we'd have to pay. I don't know how much, but I don't have anything I can pay with anyway."

They walked on for a while, both of them lost in thought.

"What does this woman actually do?" Joe asked at length.

"I'm not sure. I think she carves the spell in runes on a bone or a piece of wood. Then you take it and put it somewhere to do its work."

"Right. Well if you want to do that, what about

using the chain of my St. Christopher for payment?"

Lucy's hand went up to her throat. "We can't do that!"

"I wouldn't want to use the St. Christopher itself," Joe said quickly. "But I get enough pocket money that I'm sure I can replace the chain when I get home."

"No, definitely not!" She shook her head emphatically. "It's too special!"

Joe felt a flush of pleasure that it meant something to her. "In that case," he said, "how about the unicorn's horn? If it's so valuable, we wouldn't need much. We could grind a bit off the end. Your parents probably wouldn't even notice."

As Lucy was thinking about this, Joe saw a movement out of the corner of his eye. He turned his head. In the alleyway they were just passing, a boy taller than him, with curly blond hair, peeled himself away from the wall and disappeared between two buildings. Joe gulped.

"What's the matter?" Lucy glanced across at him, and then down the alleyway beyond. "There wasn't anyone there, was there?"

"No," Joe lied. "It's nothing." He felt a shiver run over his skin. It might not have been Thorbiorn, he told himself. He hadn't seen the boy's face. And even if it had been him, maybe the older boy hadn't heard what he'd just said to Lucy.

But why else would he have hurried away like that?

Sickness churned in Joe's stomach. Had he really just let slip the secret of the family's most precious treasure, to the worst possible person?

"Shall we go back?" he said, trying to keep his voice casual.

"Already? Why? My mother usually expects us to stay out longer than this."

"You don't think she and your father have gone out as well and left the house empty, do you?"

"I doubt it. There's almost always someone at home, even when nobody's in the workshop."

"Well, just in case, I think we should go back anyway."

Lucy looked at him, bewildered. "I don't understand you sometimes! One minute, you're suggesting we should grind off some of the horn, which would mean waiting until everyone's out. And the next minute you're worrying in case there's no-one there!"

"Please."

"Alright!" She rolled her eyes. "We'll go back this way then."

They set off back towards Coppergate at a pace which seemed to Joe painfully slow. In his mind, he repeated the same words over and over. *It wasn't him. He didn't hear. Everything will be alright. It wasn't him. He didn't hear. Everything will be alright.*

He only hoped it would be true.

11

Lokki and Mattheus were in the workshop when Lucy and Joe got back. Joe felt his knees tremble with relief. Thorbiorn couldn't have slipped past them into the house, and even if he'd got in from the back yard, Lucy's father would have heard him, since the wall between the workshop and the living area was so thin.

As they were about to go inside, Aileen came running down the street, flushed and out of breath. Her basket swung wildly on her arm.

"Have you heard the news?" she cried.

"News?"

"The king is dead!" She leant against Lokki's workbench, panting. "Sigtryggr is dead!"

Lokki put down his tools and stood up. "How did it happen?"

"He had a fever, they say. They drained his blood to try and break it. But he weakened and died."

Lucy's father shook his head. "A great warrior like him, dying in his own bed! It's hard to believe!"

"What will happen now?" Lucy asked.

"No-one knows." Aileen straightened up. "He had several sons, so one of them will probably become the next king, though nobody knows which one."

"Before any of that, though," said Lokki, "there'll be the burial, most likely a ship burial for a chief like him."

Joe looked across at Lucy. Her face was alight with excitement. "Will we go?" she asked.

"Of course! The whole of Jorvik will go, and everyone from the villages around as well!" Lokki's eyes grew misty. "I haven't been to a ship burial since I was a boy. It's something you're lucky to see even once in your life."

"But we're nowhere near the sea, are we?" Joe said. "How will the ship get here?"

"It'll sail upriver, but probably not as far as Jorvik. They'll most likely moor at Staddlethorpe, just before the river narrows. That's where we sail from in the spring and autumn."

"How do we get there?" Lucy asked.

"Horse and cart." Lokki scratched his beard. "Mattheus, you'll need to go out to Haxby to fetch the horse."

"Won't cousin Finwith bring it? He'll have to travel through Jorvik on his way down."

"He'll have enough to think about without running errands for us. There's going to be plenty to do, to get ready." Lokki picked up the cup he'd been working on and put it on a shelf. "That'll have to wait.

Mattheus, I need you to clean up both shields and axes, while I polish my sword and helmet. After that, we'll make Peder a new practise sword. I've got a couple of nice pieces of oak. I could make one for you, Joe, if you'd like?"

Joe beamed. "Oh yes, please!"

"There won't be fighting, will there?" Lucy said anxiously.

"Not real fighting. But there'll probably be a re-enactment of Sigtryggr's most famous battle. We'll see if we can afford to get you a helmet, Mattheus. You ought really to have something before the next raid anyway."

"With horns on?" Joe burst out in excitement.

At once, everyone turned to look at him. "Why would you have horns on a helmet?" Lokki looked perplexed.

"To disguise yourself as a cow, maybe!" Mattheus grinned.

Joe blushed. "I thought you did," he mumbled.

"You'd never be able to hold your head up under the weight, lad." Lokki turned to his wife. "Have we woven enough fabric for any of you to have a new cloak?"

"There's not much yet," she said, "after the ones I made for you and Mattheus last year. But there might be enough for Luiseach or Aine."

Lokki paced around his workshop. "The best clothes will need to be washed too. And if I sell one of the plates in the chest, we can probably all have new shoes, as well as a helmet for Mattheus."

"Don't we need to offer something for the burial treasure?"

Lokki nodded. "There are three silver plates. We can offer one, sell one to someone who needs an offering, and still keep one." He clapped his hands. "We need to get started. Luiseach, do you know where your brother and sisters are? We need them back here to help."

"Joe and I will fetch them." Lucy tugged Joe out on to the street again. "We'll be back in a few minutes!" she called over her shoulder as she rushed away up Coppergate.

Joe hurried to keep up with her. At the end of the track, Lucy paused. "You know which way Peder went?" she said. "From here, it's down there, first track on the left, over the crossroads. Then it's the second to last house on the right."

"You're not coming?" Joe felt his stomach tighten.

"I'm going to get Sorcha and Aine."

"But what if Peder's not there, at his friend's house?"

Lucy squeezed his arm. "If they've gone out, Bernhard's mother, Guthrun, will know where they've gone. See you back at our house." She gave him a brief smile and dashed off in the opposite direction.

For a second, Joe stood and watched her disappear. He knew it was daft to worry about being left on his own for a few minutes. When he arrived back in Lucy's world yesterday morning, he'd waited a couple of hours for her, he reminded himself. Yesterday. Had he really only been here for a day? It seemed so much longer.

He set off down the track, the way Lucy had pointed, and then took the first left. As he reached the crossroads, he stopped automatically to look left and right, just as he would if he were crossing a road at home.

Suddenly, he felt his upper arm clamped in a grip that was painfully tight.

"There you are!" snarled a voice in his ear.

He twisted round. It was Thorbiorn. He didn't let go of Joe.

"Were you following me?" Joe asked through gritted teeth.

"Not exactly. Though I did happen to be coming along Coppergate a few moments ago, in time to see you leaving with my cousin. We're going this way." He dug his thumb hard into the muscle underneath Joe's arm.

Joe winced and pulled away. "I was going over there, actually."

"It'll hurt much less if you come with me," crooned Thorbiorn. He pushed Joe down the track he'd been about to cross.

"What do you want this time?" Joe turned his ankle in a rut and stifled a yelp.

"To start with, somewhere to talk where we won't be overheard," hissed Thorbiorn, "though it's true the town is in such a flutter, nobody's likely to take much notice of us." He tightened his grip on Joe's arm and pushed him onwards faster. Unable to sidestep the frozen puddles, Joe slithered and slipped on the ice.

For a couple of minutes, they continued in this way. Then Thorbiorn said, "Here! This will do nicely."

They had come to an open stretch of ground beside the river. Thorbiorn pushed Joe down on to his knees. Joe glanced around, praying that someone would come by and stop the older boy from whatever he was about to do. But they hadn't passed anyone on the track, and there was nobody to be seen now. Thorbiorn had chosen his spot well. They were some distance from either of the bridges, and there were long back yards between them and the nearest buildings.

He let go of Joe's arm and stepped back, pulling his knife from his belt.

Joe was aware of his heart pounding. People always said you should hide your fear. But it was easier said than done, he found. "What do you want?" he asked again.

Thorbiorn tilted the knife this way and that, watching the dull light from the sky glint on the blade.

"I want to know how you do it," Thorbiorn said softly.

"How I do what?"

"How you appear and disappear."

Joe frowned. "I don't."

Thorbiorn ran his thumb across the blade of the knife. "Don't pretend to be stupid," he said, twisting his mouth into the shape of a smile. "This -" he flicked the knife - "was on your neck last time we talked. And then you vanished, right in front of me." He took a step towards Joe. "How did you do it?"

Joe made himself keep completely still, though every instinct screamed at him to run away. "You made it happen," he said, trying to sound calm. "You threatened me. That's what happens when I'm in danger."

"Hah! Of course you'd say that! You won't trick me that easily!"

"But it's true!"

"Shall we try it then?" Thorbiorn took another step forward. His eyes flashed.

This time, Joe cringed away from him.

"Before we put it properly to the test," Thorbiorn said, in the voice of a father reasoning with a child, "I'll give you one more chance to tell me how you really do it. And how you make yourself reappear? It's a very useful skill. You can be in and out of people's houses without them ever knowing you were there. Why, you could even poison someone's dogs right under their noses!"

"So it *was* you that did that! They guessed, you know!"

"Me? Did I say that? No, I just heard it had

happened." Thorbiorn polished his knife with his cuff, apparently thoughtful. "I'd say it was much more likely to be you. I'll bet there was a moment last night when you weren't being watched. You just slipped out. In fact, maybe you didn't even have to do that! That would be better still, if you could be in two places at once!"

"I can't! And I didn't poison the dogs!" Joe scrambled to his feet and staggered backwards away from Thorbiorn. For a split second, the older boy looked surprised. Then he sprang forward and knocked Joe down again. The side of Joe's face throbbed with the blow. He lay on the frozen ground, dazed.

"Let's see if it works then, your disappearing trick!" Thorbiorn crouched over him, pinning the brooch on Joe's cloak to his shoulder with the point of the knife. "Would they even miss you, if I did kill you?" he snarled.

His elbow pressed down on Joe's windpipe. Joe began to choke. If he wasn't pulled back into his own world, this time he was sure he would die. There was no reason for Thorbiorn not to kill him.

He closed his eyes and thought of Mum and Dad. He hadn't said goodbye to them. He wanted to say that he loved them. A hissing sound filled the air. It grew louder and louder in his ears. Behind it was noise, voices, confusion. The world went dark.

"Joe? Joe! Can you hear me?" It was Dad.

Joe opened his eyes. His father's face was

looking down at him, worried.

"Are you alright, Joe? What happened?"

He lifted his head. The pain pounded against his skull.

"Hold the train!" his father yelled over his shoulder. "We need to get on!"

Sam grabbed Joe's hand. "Come on!" He pulled him up.

Joe felt himself sway on his feet. He clung to Sam's arm and watched blankly as the rail guard trotted down the station platform towards them.

"Is the young man ill? I'd advise you not to board the train if he needs medical attention."

"I don't think he does," Dad said, taking Joe's other arm firmly.

Joe winced. Dad was squeezing in just the same place as Thorbiorn had done.

"Sorry, Joe." He loosened his grip. "He was fine a moment ago," he said to the guard. "I think he just came over a bit faint. Not enough breakfast, probably."

The guard looked at Joe through narrowed eyes. "Well," he said without sympathy, "if you're going, you need to hurry up and get on."

Joe leaned on Dad as they shuffled to the open doors of the train.

"Bring his bag, would you, Sam?"

Joe blundered up the steps. He felt nauseous. Now would not be a good time to be sick.

"Wait here with our stuff, you two," Dad said.

"I'll just go and find our seats."

Joe slumped down on the pull-down seat in the lobby between the carriages.

"What was all that about?" Sam asked.

"I don't know," Joe muttered. "What happened?"

"One moment, you were standing there, waiting to get on. And the next moment, you'd keeled over on top of the bags."

"Right." Joe rubbed his head. The side of it was still throbbing. "I must have fainted, I suppose." He fell silent. Sam got his phone out of his pocket again and went back to playing whatever game had been obsessing him before. It seemed to Joe as though he'd been playing it for days.

After a couple of minutes, Dad came back. "We're down this way. I'll take your stuff, Joe. If you can just get yourself as far as our seats, I'll go and find you a drink of water. You can have a good long rest all the way down to London."

Joe swayed along the train behind Dad, steadying himself on the seats on either side. He felt physically much more drained this time than he'd been before. It was hard, too, being surrounded by people straight away. When he'd come back from visiting Lucy at Fishbourne, he'd been alone each time. Even last time in York, he'd had a few seconds to gather his wits before he caught up with Dad and Sam.

He settled into his seat and closed his eyes, glad to shut out the rest of the world. There was a lot to think about: Thorbiorn and his threats, the poisoned dogs, the unicorn's horn, the dead king, what Lucy would say when he didn't come back for a second time. His brain whirled through all these things, muddling them and knitting them back together in a way that was more like a dream than like being awake.

Gradually, he came to his senses. Above all, he was relieved to have escaped Thorbiorn again. But he also felt a pang of regret that he was going to miss the ship burial. Events like that only came along once in a lifetime, Lokki had said, and that was if you were living in the right time to begin with. He would have been the only person alive today to have witnessed such a thing first hand. Of course, the fact that he could never share it with anyone would have robbed it of some of its enjoyment. But even so, he was sad that he would have to make do with looking it up in a book or on the internet.

At some point, he drifted off to sleep. He was woken by his father shaking him just as the train was coming into Kings Cross.

"Feeling any better?" Dad asked.

"A bit." Joe rubbed his eyes. In a way, he did. Lucy's world had receded and his head felt clearer. On the connecting train home from Waterloo, he ate the chocolate Dad had bought and turned the pages of the book he would usually be reading. When he got home, he decided, he would go down to the library and see what books they had about Viking times, especially

Jorvik.

Mum was waiting at the station when the train pulled in. She hugged Joe and Sam tightly. "Did you have a lovely time?" she said in the bright voice she used whenever she talked about Dad, or things they'd done with him.

"It was great!" Joe said enthusiastically.

"Yeah," said Sam. "It was cool." His phone was still in his hand.

"Delivered back to you," Dad said. "All safe and sound."

Joe looked up at his father. His face was set in a tight smile. "I'll see you in a couple of weeks then, boys." He hugged them both, then picked up his bag.

"I love you," Joe said quietly, so that Sam wouldn't hear.

Dad swallowed. "And I love you, Joe." He hugged him again, then turned and walked away to the bus stop.

"Can't we give him a lift?" Joe said to Mum. A hard lump had formed in his throat at the sight of Dad walking away.

"He'd probably rather we didn't." She led the way to the car. "Did you do lots of exciting things? What was the apartment like? You must have had fairly decent weather. It was nice here!" All the way home, she chatted. Sam had withdrawn into his phone again, so Joe did his best to answer for both of them. These conversations were always awkward because it felt disloyal to admit to Mum that they'd had a nice time without her. A couple of times, he kicked Sam to answer, but his brother only grunted.

That evening, when Joe was getting into his pyjamas, Mum came into his room and sat down on the bed. Joe braced himself. This was what she did when she wanted to ask him difficult questions, like how he was feeling at the moment, and whether there was anything he wanted to talk about. He pulled on his pyjama top and put his clothes on the chest of drawers.

"I was doing a bit of tidying while you were away," Mum said. Joe looked up, surprised. She didn't usually start like this. "I found this, down behind the printer."

She held out a piece of paper to him.

On it was the letter he'd typed to himself from Fishbourne, saying they'd found his St. Christopher and were sending it back. He swallowed. He'd been so careful, even going to the trouble of getting his ink pad out to put a blurred postmark across the stamp so he could drop the envelope through the door along with the post. But he remembered now that the printer hadn't seemed to work, and he'd set it to print a second time.

Mum was watching his face. "Can you explain how a letter like that came to be behind the printer?"

Before he could answer, she went on, "Come to that," she was looking at his neck, "where is your St. Christopher now?"

12

Joe felt colour flood into his face. He turned away quickly and bent down to put his shoes straight while he tried to think what to say. Lying made him deeply uncomfortable, especially lying to Mum. It was something that she and Dad had always been really strict about, and until he started time travelling, he'd had no trouble sticking to the truth most of the time. But there was no way he could tell her what had actually happened to his St. Christopher.

"I wrote the letter from Fishbourne," he said, hanging his head. "I found the St. Christopher caught up inside my clothes when we got home that day. I thought you'd be cross, so I made up that letter and pretended to send it back. I didn't know the printer had done two copies."

Mum frowned. "But that was weeks after we went there! You'd started back at school. Why did you wait so long? Sam said Dad gave you grief over losing it when you were staying with him. If you had it all the time, why didn't you tell him so?"

"I don't know." Joe stared at the carpet.

"And where is it now?"

"Now?" He didn't look at her. If he said it was in one of his pockets, or he hadn't yet unpacked it from his luggage, she'd want him to find it and show it to her. Then he had a brainwave. "I fainted on York station and the chain got broken. Dad took it away with him to get a new one."

"You fainted? He didn't mention that."

Joe was relieved to see he'd distracted her from the original question.

"He really ought to have said something." She sounded annoyed.

"It was nothing!" Joe said hastily. "I didn't eat enough breakfast, and then I stood up too quickly. I'm fine, really. He probably didn't want to worry you."

"I'd still prefer to know. Has it happened before?"

"No. It was just a silly thing, honestly. It's fine, really it is." He tried to think of a way of changing the subject. "Can I go to the library tomorrow?"

She shook her head. "It's closed on Sundays. Why? What did you want to look at?"

"Nothing much." He shrugged. "We went to the Viking Centre in York, that's all. It was sort of interesting."

Mum stood up. "So we're on to Vikings now, are we? I'm glad we're moving through history in chronological order!" She smiled and stroked his hair.

"Go and clean your teeth. I'll be up again in a bit to say goodnight." She went off downstairs.

Since he couldn't go to the library, Joe spent over an hour the following day searching the internet for anything about the king of York's burial. He'd found the right king, he was fairly sure - a man who the Vikings called Sigtryggr had been king of Dublin and then king of York, and had died some time in 927. There was even something about him becoming a Christian, and then changing his mind, like Lucy had said.

But there was nothing about his burial. Joe was sure Lokki had mentioned Staddlethorpe, and 'thorpe' did seem to be part of Viking place names. But there wasn't a place with that name any more, only a road called Staddlethorpe Broad Lane. He peered at the map. It did lead down to the River Ouse, just at the point where it narrowed, like Lokki had said. So perhaps that was the spot. Even if it was, though, he couldn't find anything about a Viking ship burial nearby. There were only three altogether for the whole of Britain, two in Scotland and one on the Isle of Man. Joe was puzzled. Perhaps Lokki had been wrong, and Sigtryggr hadn't been given a ship burial after all.

After school on Monday, he went to the library and borrowed all the books he could find on Vikings. He knew that if he couldn't find anything on the internet, there wasn't likely to be anything in the books. But there might be other things that would be useful to know if he got back into Lucy's time again.

A lot of the books focused on battles and voyages, however, and most of the rest were about stuff he knew already. The only bits that were new were explanations of things he'd come across while he was there. Ice skates were made of bone, he found, and the bread was gritty because it had tiny specks of rock in it, from the stones used to grind the flour. There was something about unicorn horns too - they were actually the tusk of a kind of whale called a narwhal. So Lucy's grandfather had probably caught a narwhal himself and sawn its horn off, and then lied about it, or he'd bought it from someone else who had done just that. Joe found himself strangely irritated that Lucy should have been taken in so completely.

All in all, he felt rather grumpy. He tried, as he'd often done before, to forget all about Lucy's time. But over the next two weeks, he found it hard to concentrate. It seemed that no matter what he was doing, whether it was working on a comprehension exercise for homework, or splashing along muddy tracks for cross country, a part of his brain was imagining Lucy and the others making their preparations for the king's burial. The big event, whatever it was, would all be over by the time he went back, if he actually managed to get back again. It was hard not to feel he was missing out.

"Mum says you've been looking at stuff about Vikings," Dad said, when Joe and Sam went to stay with him for the weekend again. "I'm glad the Jorvik centre inspired you."

Joe smiled politely. He couldn't very well say that it was more like thinking about somewhere you'd been on holiday and wondering what you would be doing now if you were still there.

"You know, quite a lot of words we use every day come from the Vikings," Dad said. "Really common ones like 'want' and 'get', and things like 'window' and 'husband', and 'egg'."

Joe nodded. He'd seen that in one of the library books. It was interesting in a way. But things like words and place names were just leftovers, clues for working out the past. He didn't need to do that because he'd seen it in real life.

"I was wondering," Dad said, "is there anything you'd like to do this weekend, relating to Vikings?"

"No, not really."

"Wilton isn't too far away," Dad persisted. "There was a famous battle there between the Vikings and the Anglo-Saxons. We could go and see whether there's anything to see."

Joe tried to think of a nice way of refusing. "I don't think Sam would be very happy about that," he said.

Dad grinned. "No, you're probably right there!"

So instead they played football in the park, went bowling, and ate pizza while they watched a film. Joe didn't think about Lucy at all.

On Monday morning, he was sitting at his desk listening to the teacher explaining how to do long division, when he heard a hissing sound. He looked around to see if anyone else could hear it. But the other children were looking at the numbers on the whiteboard, or staring out of the window, or fidgeting. Nobody else seemed to be hearing anything unusual.

He stuck his finger in one ear and then the other, in case there was something blocking it. But the hissing just got louder. He shook his head, but it still didn't stop. He couldn't be about to slip into Lucy's time, surely! Not in the middle of the classroom! He hadn't even been thinking about her particularly.

But then he realised he'd been thinking about how impossible it had been to do long division in Roman numerals with her brother Petrus, and then thinking about the fact that in her new world, Lucy didn't even know how many a thousand was. A moment later, he nearly fell off his chair with dizziness. He closed his eyes and held on tightly to his desk.

But his fingers grasped at thin air. The desk had gone. He took a deep breath and opened his eyes again. He was standing up, outside as far as he could tell, in darkness that was thicker and blacker than anything he had ever experienced at home.

He stretched out one arm in front of him. His fingers were faint at the end of it, just pale shapes. Cold seized them. He tucked both his hands quickly inside his cloak and pulled it tight around him. From nearby came the gentle sound of water lapping.

Beneath the stink of rubbish, he could smell the river.

He knew from every other time he'd slipped back into Lucy's world that he must have reappeared in the same place as he'd disappeared. That meant he must be on the bank of the river, where Thorbiorn had taken him.

Cautiously, he began to make his way towards the black humps of buildings, away from the river. The ground was rough, and several times he stubbed his toes against rocks he couldn't see in the dark. Each time, he hopped and rubbed his foot, then stumbled on, muttering rude words under his breath.

Quite soon, he reached the backs of the long yards behind the houses and found the track that Thorbiorn had forced him down. Though it was gloomy between the fences, he found he could see better than he'd been able to a few minutes earlier. Either his eyes were getting used to the darkness, or it was closer to dawn than he'd thought. He walked up the track, doing his best to avoid the icy puddles in the ruts.

He came to a crossroads and hesitated. He'd been about to cross straight over when Thorbiorn had caught hold of him. So to retrace his steps, he should turn left here, then right at the next junction, and then Coppergate would be on his left. He felt pleased with himself for remembering the way. Previously, all of Jorvik had looked much the same to him, but his brain seemed at last to be making sense of the town.

At Lucy's house, he hesitated again. A few

shadowy figures had hurried by as he was walking, but he guessed it must still be extremely early. The household was probably fast asleep. He blew on his hands and shifted from foot to foot, wondering if there was a way to keep himself warm while he waited for dawn.

Suddenly, the door opened. Joe sprang back just in time to avoid having a bucket of dirty water slopped over him.

"Joe?"

He looked up. Lucy stood in the doorway with the now empty bucket.

"Is that you?" she asked. "You're back! Where have you been? How did you know?"

"How did I know what?"

"We're leaving as soon as it's light. We thought we'd have to go without you!"

"Without me?"

"Well, it would have been your own fault! If you wanted to come, you shouldn't have disappeared for two days!"

"Two days?" He stared at her.

"Would you stop repeating everything I say!" She was obviously exasperated but she sounded excited too. "The burial is tonight, at Howden. It'll take us four hours, five if the roads are bad. Father decided we should leave at dawn, so we have time to set up camp."

"You mean the king of Jorvik's burial?"

"Who else?" She stepped back into the house. "Do you want some breakfast? There's probably a little bit left in the pot."

Joe followed her, still bewildered. "I haven't missed it then?"

"No! Like I said, you're just in time to come with us. But I do wish you wouldn't keep disappearing like that!"

To Joe's surprise, it was hive of activity in the main room of the house, as each person helped with the last preparations for the journey.

"Look who I found on the street!" Lucy called out.

"Well, I never!" exclaimed Aileen. "Are you alright, Joe? We were worried about you when Peder came back on his own."

Joe grinned sheepishly. "It was Thorbiorn again," he said. "He grabbed me just after Lucy left me - I mean Luiseach," he corrected himself. "He dragged me down to the river and pulled his knife again."

"But you got away?" Lucy's eyes were gratifyingly wide.

"Yes, but I didn't dare come back immediately."

Lokki stopped what he was doing. "You should have done! We would have protected you!"

"I know. I'm sorry." Joe hung his head.

"Never mind. You're here now. We'll add a bit to the provisions. I'm afraid I didn't make you a sword or shield, though. You'll have to use Peder's old ones. Get them out, please, Peder!"

"Thank you. Can I do anything to help?"

Lokki put another loop of the rope around the bundle he was tying up. "Eat something first, while Mattheus brings the horse and cart round from the yard, and then you can help us load up."

Joe guessed it was getting on for two hours later by the time they were finally on their way. Lokki had been chafing and fretting from the time it began to get light, but there seemed to be an incredible number of packages and parcels of all different sizes to be loaded on to the cart, including the great chest of clothes Aileen had opened last time Joe was there. And then each member of the family remembered something they had forgotten to pack, or something they had forgotten to do. Joe stood beside the horse, since he had no preparations of his own to make, watching them running in and out of the house. It was just like his own family getting ready to go away on their annual camping holiday. He smiled to himself, before he remembered that there wouldn't be any more family holidays with Mum and Dad together.

Finally, everything was loaded, and everyone had found a space somewhere. Joe wondered whether the horse would be able to move the cart at all, but at Lokki's flick of the reins, it plodded forward a few steps.

Coppergate was now thronging with people, however. Donkeys and ponies, and even goats were being loaded up, and those that were ready were edging towards the junction at the end of the track. Lokki steered their horse into the line, and they inched forward.

Half an hour later, they still hadn't reached the city walls. Joe wriggled to try and get more comfortable. It was exactly like trying to get out of the car park after some big event, with hundreds of vehicles converging on one exit. So much for traffic jams being a modern invention, he thought.

At last, they were out of the city and into open country. Lokki sat up straight and flicked his birch switch against the horse's flank. The animal picked up speed and began to jog along the track which led south.

In front of them, a line of horses and carts stretched out as far as Joe could see. To the left, he recognised the copse where he had collected wood with Lucy on his last visit. He turned to look back at the walls of Jorvik, rising up behind them like some kind of computer image from a film. Horses and carts were still streaming out through the gates in the city wall, down the track. He pinched himself. It was real. He was really here.

"That took a lot longer than I hoped," Lokki called over his shoulder. "At least we're on our way now."

"Along with the rest of the country, by the look of it," said Mattheus.

Joe looked at Lucy beside him. Her eyes were shining.

"I'm glad you didn't miss it!" she whispered.

13

It seemed to take forever to get to Howden. Joe thought he remembered seeing it on the map, closer to York than Staddlethorpe Broad Lane, which itself had only been about twenty-five miles away. But the horse didn't go that much quicker than they could have walked, and they had to stop several times to dig the cartwheels out of the mud.

By the time they arrived, it was mid afternoon. Joe stirred himself and looked around. They were in the middle of an enormous field with a river running along the bottom of it. There was nothing else here, no village or building of any kind, only an encampment of tents which was growing larger as more and more people arrived.

He climbed down, stretching and yawning, surprised at how tired he was from the journey. He was also stiff with cold. What would be really nice now, he thought, would be a long, hot bath, or at least a mug of hot chocolate in front of a fire to help him warm up. Instead, there was grass and frozen mud, and no shelter from the open skies or the wind that whipped across the field.

Aileen stamped her feet and blew on her hands. "Right, Aine and Peder, I want you to get the buckets down from the cart and fetch water from the river. Luiseach and Joe, go and ask someone for some embers. Those families over there have been here longest." She pointed. "Take this pot, and make sure they don't go out on the way back. Sorcha, please can you lay the fire with the wood we brought, so it's ready to light as soon as they come back. Mattheus and I will help your father to get the shelter up."

Joe set off with Lucy towards the end of the field Aileen had indicated. "How does she know those people have been here longest?" he asked, yawning again. "Lots of other families have got their tents up." He gestured at the groups of people dotted around the field unloading their possessions from their carts. In between the finished camps, the latest arrivals were busy constructing A-frame tents, with the pair of diagonals at each end joined by a ridge pole, all held together by a rectangular structure around the bottom. Once the frames were ready, they tied sheets of thick, cream-coloured material on to them, and pegged them to the frozen ground.

Lucy looked around. "I suppose if you'd arrived first," she said, "you'd choose the best spot to set up your shelter."

"And that's all the way over there, is it?"

She grinned. "Well, they've got the only place that's not windy, in the lee of the hedgerow. So yes, it is."

"Oh. I see. But that still doesn't explain why their fire is better than anyone else's."

"Yes it does. The longer the fire's been lit, the hotter it's likely to be. And the easiest way to light a fire is to use embers or burning charcoal from another fire that's really hot."

"You don't use matches, then?"

Lucy looked blank. "Matches?"

"Never mind."

She paused to speak to someone she knew. Joe waited. As they walked on, she waved to another family. "Isn't it exciting?" she said, her face glowing. "I've never been to anything like this before!"

"Me neither," Joe said. "I've seen big camps a bit like this, but not quite the same. Do you know a lot of these people?"

"About half of them, I think. It seems funny to travel such a long way and then see so many people from home."

They came to a tent with a roaring fire outside. There was a big, black pot over it, just like at Lucy's house. Joe hung back while she approached. A few moments later, she came out with a man Joe recognised as the host from the storytelling evening.

He guffawed loudly at something Lucy had said, then picked up a large pair of tongs and plucked two red hot pieces of charcoal from the fire. "Ready, young lady?" He dropped them into the pot Lucy held out. "No stopping to gossip on your way back, now!" He grinned, and went back inside his tent.

Joe and Lucy hurried back across the field together. Joe was amazed to see that the tent was up already. For some reason, he'd expected it to take much longer than a modern tent. It was also surprisingly large. Inside, Aileen was spreading furs over a ground sheet at one end and there were two trestles in the middle, balancing a short piece of wood which acted as a makeshift table. Sorcha took the charcoal from Lucy and bent down to the fire she had laid in front of the tent, sheltering it from the wind with one hand while she coaxed the kindling to light. Lokki and Mattheus carried on lifting down the rest of the luggage from the cart.

From all around the field, despite the wind, Joe could hear a hum of excitement.

"There'll just be time to finish setting up before we have to wash and change," Lokki said, as he and Mattheus carried the chest of clothes into the tent.

"What time does it begin?" Lucy asked.

"Dusk."

"Where do we wash?" asked Joe.

"In the river."

Joe shuddered. He was still quite cold, and bathing in icy water sounded like a terrible idea. He wondered what would happen if he got ill here. It would be hard to explain back at home how he'd caught pneumonia sitting in the classroom.

For the next little while, Lokki and Aileen kept everyone busy with jobs. Extra lengths of fabric were hung over the walls on the inside of the tent to make it warmer, and all of the family's possessions were stowed away as neatly as possible, just like setting up camp on Joe's own family holidays. The cooking pot was hung over the fire outside, on the stand they had brought from home, and once the fire was hot, two large pots of tallow were nestled into the flames at the edge. Lokki brought out a dozen long sticks which had already been wound round at one end with rope. As soon as the tallow had melted, he set Joe and Peder to dipping the roped ends in the hot liquid. Joe gazed into the flames, glad to be given a job that allowed him to stand where it was warm.

When at last he went with Lokki to wash in the river, he was relieved to find that he was only expected to splash his face, hands and arms, though Lokki and Mattheus immersed their whole heads to rinse their hair. Back at the tent, Aileen and the girls had bathed and dressed already, and were busy fastening their best brooches and putting on make-up. Joe changed quickly into the same set of clothes he'd worn for the storytelling evening and sat down in a corner to wait.

Presently, there was a faint beating sound in the distance. Everyone around him looked up, listening.

"The ship has arrived," Aileen murmured.

"It's time to go," Lokki said. He handed Mattheus his new helmet, put on his own, and picked up the bundle of dipped sticks. Keeping one for himself, he gave one each to Aileen and Mattheus and put the rest in a bag slung over his shoulder beneath his cloak.

"Have you got the dish?" Aileen asked.

Lokki nodded. He thrust the end of his stick into the fire. There was a spitting sound and a flare of brightness as the tallowed rope caught light. He lifted it, burning, into the air. Aileen and Mattheus did the same. All around the field in the half-light, flames were springing up.

Then from every part of the encampment, the flickering lights began to move towards the river and the sound of the drums. Lucy's family fell into line, with Lokki and Mattheus at the head, followed by Sorcha and Peder. Aileen came next, holding Aine's hand, while Joe and Lucy walked quietly side by side at the back.

Joe tried hard to notice and remember every detail: the bobbing flames, the muted sound of so many people moving in near silence together, the bite of sharp cold in the air, the cry of seabirds high above them, drifting inland for the night. And behind it, always, the insistent beat of the drums.

Soon, he could see a warm glow ahead. On the bank of the river were two enormous bonfires. Moored between them, with its prow to the shore, was a Viking longship. Its proud, carved head reared up at the front, and from the centre, its graceful mast reached high into the violet sky. Firelight glinted on the circles of shields set out along the side of the boat, and beneath them, its curved hull bristled with oars. Joe felt his heart skip a beat. The ship was more beautiful and more impressive than he could ever have imagined.

As the torchlight procession reached the nearer of the two bonfires, the people at the front began to form a straight line that led inland away from the bank of the river. People coming from the opposite direction did the same. The torches were making a corridor of light, Joe realised. He took his place beside Lucy and a tingle of excitement shivered through him.

On the ground between the two lines lay the felled trunks of what Joe guessed must be a hundred tall, straight trees, arranged crossways like the steps of a ladder. After a few minutes, the drums stopped. In silence, the men handed their torches and shields to their wives and children, and stepped forward. As one, they moved down towards the river past the ends of the tree trunks. When they reached the bank, they didn't stop, but stepped out into the freezing, black water to surround the ship. Joe glanced at his friend. She stood with her mouth open, entranced.

The oars were drawn in, and each man took up a rope from beside the hull and put it over his shoulder. Then the drums began again, marking out a slow, steady rhythm this time. It was clearly a signal, because with every fourth beat, there came a sound that was something between a growl and a roar as the men strained together against the ship's colossal weight. Inch by inch, they hauled the mighty vessel forward, out of the water and up the shore, the trunks of the trees rolling beneath its hull as it moved.

Joe watched Lokki and Mattheus pass him, the arteries in their faces standing out like ropes as they heaved and sweated. At last, the prow of the ship reached the darkness at the top of the line and the drumming changed rhythm once more. Joe leaned forward to try to see what was happening. The ship began to tip very slightly and then a little more, as the men at the front lowered the bow into a shallow pit that had been dug out of the ground. The drums stopped, and there were shouts that Joe couldn't understand. Then, even more slowly than before, the men dragged the ship forward and down into the pit.

Behind them, the older boys carried the last of the tree trunks away. A group of women encircled an immense pile of wood beyond the prow and drove their torches into the heart of it, setting it alight. From the river's edge, the two sides of the blazing corridor came together as people moved in a mass towards the ship.

Joe and Lucy edged forward with everyone else. The mast was lowered, and gradually, the sound of the drumming grew louder. A whisper rippled through the crowd. Joe looked around to see what was happening. From some distance away, on the hillside above them, a bright knot of light had emerged from the darkness, followed by a line of torches like a string of fairy lights.

"It's him!" Lucy whispered. "It's the king!"

As the light approached the edge of the crowd, Joe could just make out six men carrying a kind of stretcher on their shoulders. It had upright poles at each corner which supported a canopy over the body, like the drapes on a four-poster bed. Despite the light cast by the torch bearers who flanked the stretcher, it was too dark to see much of the great man himself.

Behind, a young woman stumbled along, weeping loudly and bound at the wrist to a man. They in turn were followed by a line of men and women leading horses, bullocks, and dogs towards the ship.

The crowd parted, and the stretcher bearers boarded the boat and lifted the body of the king on to a kind of bed. About half the men who had dragged the vessel up from the river then stepped forward, Lokki among them. Light shone on the silver dish he brought out from the bag beneath his cloak. He leaned over the side of the ship and placed it beside the dead king. The other men, too, made their offerings.

As Lokki moved away, Joe watched the weeping woman step on to the boat. The bonds at her wrist were cut and she knelt beside the king's body, wailing. Behind her, the animals were also led up the gangplank on to the ship.

Joe tugged Aileen's sleeve. "What happens to all of them?" he whispered.

Lucy's mother looked down at him. "They go with King Sigtryggr into the afterlife," she murmured.

"Is the woman his wife?"

"No, she's his favourite female slave."

"So what does she do? How can she go with him?"

Before Aileen could answer, Joe suddenly knew what she was going to say. He felt the hairs stand up on the back of his neck.

"She'll be sacrificed," Aileen whispered, "along with the animals."

Joe shivered. "They kill her?"

Aileen nodded.

"But that's horrible!" Tears had sprung in Lucy's eyes.

"Hush!" Aileen put her hand gently on her daughter's head. In spite of the glow from the torches all around, she herself looked pale. "That's the custom," she whispered. She reached out and pulled Joe and Lucy close to her skirts.

"Will she be buried alive?" Lucy asked between sobs.

"No. An old woman will come. They call her the Angel of Death. She'll kill the girl quickly and cleanly so that she doesn't suffer."

"But she's suffering already!" Joe protested.

"She knows what's going to happen! That's why she's crying, isn't it? She's not sad about the king. She's terrified!"

Aileen squeezed his shoulder. "She volunteered," she said gently. "She may be afraid now, but she asked to be chosen for this. It's a great honour."

The crowd stirred again as the drummers moved forward. They boarded the ship and formed a line down both sides, shoulder to shoulder with the other men already on the boat. The king, the young woman and the animals were all hidden from view.

An old woman shuffled forward, bent over her walking stick.

"That's her, isn't it! The Angel of Death!" Lucy buried her face in Aileen's side. "I can't watch!"

The old woman made her way slowly up the gangplank. For the briefest moment, Joe thought he heard the weeping of the young woman change to a scream. Then the drumming rose to a deafening level, drowning out her cries.

He closed his eyes and wished passionately that he was back in the classroom at home.

14

At last, the thunderous noise broke off. The seconds of silence that followed were eerie. Then, gradually, a murmur of voices began. For a moment, Joe wondered whether this was the beginning of the hissing. Perhaps he was slipping back into his own time. He opened his eyes, hopefully. But there was no classroom to be seen. He was still here with Lucy, in the middle of the burning Viking night. Only now, the young woman who'd been led on to the ship a few minutes ago must be dead. He felt sick.

The crowd around them began to melt away, back towards the bonfires beside the river.

"What happens now?" Peder asked.

"There's a big celebration," Lokki said, as he rejoined them. He lifted his helmet for a moment and ran his hand through his hair. Sweat was still dripping down his forehead. He took back his torch and his shield. "Later on, there'll be a re-enactment of the Battle of Kylmehauog, when Sigtryggr killed Niall Glundub to become King of Dublin. You and Joe will fight beside me and Mattheus."

Joe said nothing. His insides felt frozen by what he had just witnessed. How could anyone think of celebrating when they had just watched a murder? He was appalled.

He followed Lucy's family as they moved back towards the river with the rest of the crowd. Beside him, Lucy was silent too.

"What about the burial itself?" Peder was asking. "When does that happen?"

"Just before dawn," Lokki replied. "Every family will have brought shovels. Ours are still at the encampment. One of us will go and fetch them in a few hours. Then everyone, man, woman and child, takes a turn moving the earth."

They reached the bonfires beside the river. Between them, beside the place where the ship had been moored, vast barrels had been set up on tables. Women in bright-edged pinafores were busy filling drinking horns with ale and mead, and passing them round. Everywhere, people talked and laughed together, helping themselves to the food that was carried through on trays. Joe stared at them. If Lokki was right, almost no-one would ever have been to a ship burial before. And yet, they were behaving as if this were an ordinary party. They seemed completely untouched by what had just happened.

He and Lucy sat quietly with Aine on a bench while Aileen went to find them something to eat.

Around the edge of the crowd, he noticed, stood tall frames, rather like candelabras, where people could stand their torches so that they had both hands free. Some had already started to burn out. He remembered Lokki putting the rest of the tallowed sticks in his bag. He'd wondered why. But if they only lasted a couple of hours, they would need quite a few for the whole night.

While he was thinking about this, his attention was caught by a shadowy figure prowling around the outside of the gathering. The boy wasn't carrying a torch himself, and he didn't seem to be eating or drinking anything, nor speaking to anyone.

Joe nudged Lucy. "Is that ...?"

"Thorbiorn," she whispered, nodding. "Let's hope he doesn't notice us."

For a few seconds, they both held their breath. Then Thorbiorn moved off into the crowd, following in Aileen's footsteps.

After a while, Lucy's mother returned with food for them all. Joe hadn't realised how hungry he was until he began to eat. He tucked in to the salted cod and honey-roast vegetables gladly, and was about to say that the food was much tastier than anything he'd previously eaten here, before he stopped himself. Aileen would think him rude and ungrateful.

From somewhere down near the river, the sound of pipes and drums carried over the heads of the crowd to where Joe and Lucy were sitting. Lucy had finished her fish and now crammed her berry pancake into her mouth.

"Can we go and see what's going on over there?" she asked her mother.

"Of course. Just make sure that you and Joe stick together. I'll take Aine with me."

Joe licked his fingers. Now that he had a full stomach, he felt better. Somehow, the burial ritual was starting to fade in his mind. It wasn't that he'd forgotten anything about it. But clearly, dwelling on it wouldn't change it. Anyway, there would be plenty of time for thinking it all over later, when he was back at home. In the meantime, it would be a shame to miss out on everything else that was happening here tonight.

"Come on!" Lucy was tugging his sleeve. "Let's go."

Joe followed her through the crowd. Most of the food had been eaten now, but the grown-ups were still standing around, drinking and laughing. Some were starting to sing. Between the bonfires was a group of people clustered together. Joe and Lucy crept through to find that they were watching a wrestling match. There was a lot of shouting and cheering, and both men and women were making bets on who would win. They watched for a few minutes, then squeezed out again.

Further on, perched on a stool, was the same storyteller they had heard at Inga's house, spinning more tales to the adults and children who sat around him, listening with rapt attention. Beyond him, was someone juggling with three flaming torches.

"Look at that!" breathed Lucy, in awe. "Have you ever seen anything like it?"

Joe smiled and didn't answer. It would be churlish to say that he'd seen someone doing that every time he'd been to Covent Garden. For a moment, he really wished that he could take her back with him into his own world. There were so many things he took for granted at home that would amaze her.

After a while, there was a rallying cry to begin the re-enactment of the battle.

Joe hung back.

"Come on!" Lucy took his hand and led him forward towards the battle lines. "It'll be fun, you'll see!"

Peder and Lokki appeared at his side, and Lokki brought out two wooden swords and shields from the bag beneath his cloak. "Just remember," he bellowed over the growing commotion around them. "Nobody will hurt you, and you shouldn't hurt anyone else with your deadly weapon!"

Joe examined the sword he'd been given. The point was blunt and even in the flickering firelight, it showed the dents and scuffs of Peder's battle practice. He grinned.

"We're playing the part of the Irish," Lokki shouted, "so we need to be lying slaughtered on the field at the end."

There was a cry from further along the line, and before Joe knew what was happening, both sides of men and boys were rushing headlong at one another. For the next minute or so, he jigged around awkwardly, not sure how to move or what to do. But then another boy of about his age launched himself on to Joe. Instinctively, he raised his shield to block the attack. Then, with a blood-curdling cry, he leapt into action, thrusting and parrying, weaving and turning, his hesitation completely forgotten.

Too soon, he saw Peder and his other compatriots begin to fall. He glanced over his shoulder to check that Lucy was watching. Then he allowed his opponent to strike, and died the most theatrical death he could manage, lying hot and breathless on the hard ground.

"You must be thirsty," she said, as he staggered off the field when victory had been declared. She was carrying two large tankards of barley beer. "That was great, especially the bit when you died!" She smiled and held out his beer to him.

Joe felt himself turn pink with pride. He smiled back and took a long drink. Like the food, the beer tasted better than it had done at Lucy's house, much sweeter. A couple of minutes later, he wondered if it was stronger too. His legs felt slightly unsteady, and the world seemed to be one big, warm haze.

"Come on!" Lucy said. "I want to dance."

Joe finished off his drink. "I can't dance!" he said. "I've no idea how you do it here."

"Don't worry. You learn as you go." She dragged him towards two long lines of torches.

For a while, they stood on the edge and watched. The dancers flung themselves wildly around, laughing and whooping as they whirled past. They seemed to change partners according to some pattern Joe couldn't make out, and collided with one another quite often.

When the music stopped, they bowed and curtsied to each other. Lucy took Joe's sword and shield from him and put them down beside the torches.

"I can't do this!" he whispered. "I can't remember all those steps! We'll get trampled!"

"It'll be fine!" Lucy's eyes were shining. She pulled him into the middle of the space. "It won't be the same dance again anyway. The caller is going to tell us what to do, and then we have a practice."

Joe concentrated hard on the instructions. Fortunately, the steps were simple but he felt shy as he took Lucy's hands to walk through the pattern. As soon as the music started, however, the rhythm of the drums and the tune of the pipes made his feet twitch. He spun Lucy round and round, while she threw back her head and laughed.

At last, after a dozen dances or more, they went to sit down, exhausted. Joe wondered what time it was. He guessed it must be well past midnight by now. He yawned. Lucy yawned too.

Aileen came over. "You two look tired. You've done well to last this long. Do you want me to take you back to the camp to sleep for a while?"

Joe was about to refuse, but the thought of a bed

seemed suddenly very enticing.

"Where's Aine?" Lucy asked.

"She curled up on a rug by the fire much earlier."

"What about the burial part of the ceremony? We all have to do that, don't we?" Lucy yawned again.

"That's not for a few hours. We'll wake you when we come back to get the shovels." Aileen picked up Joe's wooden weapons, took a torch from the stand and shepherded them both down to the river path and back to the encampment.

It felt warm inside the tent after the breeze which had been blowing across the water. Joe unpinned his cloak, kicked off his shoes and sank down gratefully on the sheepskins Aileen had laid out. Within moments of pulling his blankets over him, he was fast asleep.

He was still deeply asleep when he felt someone shaking his shoulder. He groaned and tried to open his eyes. His whole body felt like lead. He let himself sink back into his dream again.

"Joe!" the voice hissed. He felt himself shaken harder.

"What?" he mumbled. "What's the matter?" He forced his eyes open. It was dark. "Where am I?" His brain felt slow and fuzzy. "Is that you, Lucy?"

"Yes. Sssh!"

He rolled over towards her voice.

"There's someone out there!" she whispered.

He closed his eyes again. "So what?"

Lucy bent down and put her mouth close to his ear. "I think they're trying to untie the horse."

"Right." He buried his face in the sheepskin.

"No, Joe!" she hissed. "It's not anyone from our family. Someone's stealing it!"

"Oh." He tried to stir himself. It seemed to take a huge effort. He sat up. "What shall we do?"

"Keep your voice down! I don't think they know that we're here." She crawled over his legs to the door flap and peeped out. "Oh no!" she muttered.

"What?"

"I think it's Thorbiorn."

"Thorbiorn?" Joe groaned, more awake now. "It would be!"

From outside the tent, there was the sound of panting and exertion as Thorbiorn hauled himself up on to the back of the horse. "You're not much of an animal, are you?" he growled. The horse shifted its hooves and snorted. "We'll see what you're really made of now!"

He must have dug his heels sharply into the animal's flanks because it gave a whinny of surprise.

"Get on then, you old nag!" Thorbiorn commanded.

With another indignant whinny, the animal turned around and trotted away through the encampment.

At once, Lucy unlooped the fastenings of the

door flap and scrambled out of the tent. "Oh goodness!" she cried. "He's thrashing the horse now! I think he's trying to get it to gallop!" She turned back to Joe, who was still sitting on his bed. "We'd better run back to the feast and tell my father." She looked miserable. "We should have stopped him!"

"What could we have done? He would have just drawn his knife on us." Joe rubbed his hand through his hair and pulled on his shoes. "The question is, where's he going in such a hurry?"

"Who knows? Back to Jorvik, I suppose."

"But why would he steal a horse in the middle of the night to ride back to Jorvik, while everyone else is still enjoying the feast?"

Lucy shrugged.

A horrible thought came to Joe. "Actually," he said, "I think I might know. There was something I didn't tell you." He avoided looking at Lucy. "When I was here before, the morning we found the dogs had been poisoned -"

"Sunday?"

He nodded. Of course, it must be more recent to Lucy than it was to him. "You know we went out, and you were telling me about the unicorn horn? Well, I thought I saw him, in the alleyway, just when we were talking about grinding the end off the horn."

"Why didn't you say something?" Her outline was dark in the doorway, but Joe could hear that she was frowning.

"I wasn't sure," he said. "Whoever it was ran off, so I didn't get a good look. In fact, it was only because he ran off that I noticed him at all. That's why I said to you we should go back, in case there was no-one at your house."

He sensed a prickling in the air. "You should have told me," Lucy said.

He looked up. Her hands were on her hips.

"I'm sorry. I hoped I was wrong. I didn't think it would come to anything."

She turned away and looked out across the encampment. Joe stood up and hovered behind her.

"Well, it's too late now," she said. "We'll have to go after him, just in case. He could be going somewhere else altogether, but I can't see why he'd decide to do that in the middle of the night." She moved briskly past Joe to pick up her cloak from her bed.

"What shall we do?" Joe asked meekly. "It'll take us hours to walk."

"We'll borrow a horse. Put your cloak on."

He did as he was told.

There was a ragged moment of moonlight. "We'll take that one down there." She pointed to a big, black horse tethered near the river. "He looks strong."

"Shouldn't we leave a note, or something?"

"A note?"

"You know, a message to say where we've gone, and that we're only borrowing the horse, not stealing it."

"There's no point! I can't write, and even if you

could, nobody would be able to read it."

"But how will they know where we are?"

"They won't. It's too bad. We haven't got time to go back to the feast and look for my father. If Thorbiorn's going to steal the unicorn horn, we have to get there as quick as we can." She broke into a run, down the field towards the river.

Joe hurried to catch her up.

"Let's hope this horse will go faster than ours," she murmured, as she unknotted the tether. "He's got to carry us both, and we have to catch up with Thorbiorn." She tied the rope deftly around the horse's head into a kind of makeshift bridle, looping the long, loose end to the other side to act as reins.

"What about a saddle?"

"We'll have to do without. Here, give me a leg up."

Joe made a platform with his hands for her to put her foot on, the way his riding teacher had done at Fishbourne. That horse had had no saddle or stirrups either. Joe remembered how much it had hurt every time he'd fallen off.

"How do I get up?" he asked anxiously.

Lucy looked down at him from high up on the back of the stallion. She walked the horse forward a couple of steps. "Try and get your foot up on that stake he was tethered to. I'll pull you up the rest."

It took three tries, while the horse grew more and more agitated, flicking its ears and stamping its feet.

Lucy made soothing noises and stroked its nose. "Come on, Joe!" she hissed. "You can do it!"

Joe could see that the animal wouldn't give him many more chances. Desperately, he launched himself from the stake, up over its back. It whinnied and shied away. He clung to Lucy and swung his leg over, gasping for breath.

"You're there! Right, now, hold on to me, and try not to grip his sides too tightly with your legs," Lucy said. She tugged the reins and gave a command, and the animal wheeled round.

Joe held on to Lucy's waist and stared straight ahead over her shoulder. He thought of Heraclio, his teacher, grinning at him, after he'd been thrown off four times in a row. His whole body tensed.

"You have to relax," Lucy said. "Otherwise, you'll frighten the horse."

Joe took a deep breath and made himself loosen his grip on Lucy and the animal.

She patted the horse's neck. "Let's get going. We've got some miles to cover." She dug her heels into its flanks. "Trot on!"

Joe held his breath. The horse started forward.

15

After a few minutes, Joe started to feel more relaxed without having to remind himself to be calm. Lucy was clearly in total command of the horse. The moment they were out of the encampment, she'd urged it to canter, which was faster than Joe had ever managed at Fishbourne. But somehow it felt easier than bouncing around on the animal's back while it trotted.

"Where did you learn to ride like this?" he called over the thudding of its hooves.

"Cousin Finwith's farm," Lucy called back. "I spent last summer up there riding the horse Thorbiorn has taken." She bent low over the horse's neck and spoke into its ear, then straightened up again. "This is a much better animal. Thorbiorn's got a plodder. He'll find it hard work to keep it going at any speed!"

After a while, there was another break in the clouds, and the moon sailed out, lighting up the landscape for a few moments before it disappeared again.

"I didn't see Thorbiorn ahead of us," Joe called. "Are you sure we're going the right way?"

"For Jorvik, yes. We're travelling north. I've checked each time we see the stars. This is the same track we came along this morning. Don't you recognise it?"

Joe squinted through the gloom. The countryside around was flat and grey, with blotches of darker grey where there were copses of trees. It stretched away into blackness on all sides.

"I think I was asleep when we came along here."

"Lucky you! Don't nod off this time, will you?"

"No chance!" He laughed, but he could feel his muscles starting to ache from the effort of keeping balanced on the horse without saddle or stirrups to help. The longest he'd ever ridden for previously was a ten minute donkey ride, where the animal had just trudged along. Already, they'd been going for at least twice as long, he guessed, maybe even longer. But there must still be an hour to go, or perhaps two, even at this speed. He shook his head and tried not to think about it.

For a long time, they rode on without speaking. Mostly, they made swift progress. The ground had frozen hard again during the night, although it was uneven in places where so many horses and carts had ploughed through earlier in the day. Now and then, the horse stumbled, and Joe clung tightly to Lucy to keep himself from falling off. A few times, too, there was deep mud beneath the frozen crust of earth. Then Lucy let the horse slow down for a few minutes. When it walked, Joe noticed that he was now able to keep his balance without even thinking about it. Perhaps Heraclio had taught him something after all.

After a while, it struck Joe that there had been no breaks in the cloud for some time. He was peering into the sky ahead of them, wondering whether it looked somehow denser than it had done before, when he felt something small and cold land on his face. He let go of Lucy's waist to brush it away. Another speck fell on the back of his hand, and then another on his cheek.

"It's snowing!" he called to Lucy in excitement.

"I know!"

He could tell from her tone that she was rolling her eyes at him.

"It's so strange! I can't see it until it lands on us."

She shifted the reins to one hand and tucked her cloak in around her. "Why's that strange? It's always like that at night, isn't it?"

"I suppose so," he said. But at home, he thought, it wasn't. Where he lived, there were street lights. And even in places he'd been to where there weren't, the snow clouds were lit up by the lights of the nearest town.

Soon, the snow was falling much more heavily and the sky was pale with the whirl of thick flakes. Lucy coaxed and wheedled the horse, but it had slowed to a trot. Joe felt himself jolted up and down in a rhythm which was quite uncomfortable.

"Can't we go a bit faster?" he called.

"The horse doesn't like it," Lucy answered. "He can't see where he's going."

Joe shivered inside his cloak. "I'm freezing."

"Me too. Still, at least Thorbiorn will be slowed down by the snow as well."

"If he actually *is* on his way back to Jorvik," Joe muttered.

All at once, it seemed to him that they must be completely mad to be doing this. Here they were, on a bitterly cold winter's night, in the middle of bleak nowhere, with not enough clothes, no map, no blankets or food, not even any water. What had he been thinking, trusting a girl younger than himself to guide them through the darkness on a stranger's horse to somewhere miles away? If the horse fell, and they couldn't ride on, they would die out here in the cold. No-one would find them until it was too late.

He shuddered. Even if Lucy managed it, and they made it to Jorvik safely, the whole reason they had set out on such a dangerous journey was to follow a boy who was bigger and older than either of them, to try to stop him from stealing something he really wanted.

In the darkness, Joe imagined the glint of the knife Thorbiorn had held at his throat twice already. Anxiety made his chest tight. He took a few deep breaths, glad that Lucy couldn't see his face.

Eventually, the snow started to fall less thickly and Lucy persuaded the horse to speed up to a canter again. The ground everywhere was white now, which made the landscape seem a little lighter.

"I think Thorbiorn's been this way," Lucy called, leaning over the horse's neck to look down as they flew over the ground. "There are hoof prints in the snow, although they're nearly covered already."

"Is it much further, do you think?"

"I'm not sure. It looks different. I don't recognise it any more."

They sped along. All around them, it was still and silent. Even the drumming of the horse's hooves was softened by the white blanket that spread over everything.

Suddenly, Lucy cried, "We're nearly there! Look!"

Ahead of them, the walls of the city seemed to hover above the snow like a dark cloud. In less than a minute, they had covered the remaining ground and arrived at the city gates.

They were shut.

The horse came to an abrupt halt. "Oh no!" Lucy half-turned to face Joe. "I hadn't thought of that! Of course, they're closed. They're always closed at night."

"But I thought everyone travelled out to the burial. Why shut them?"

"The city still needs to be secure. Otherwise the

people of Jorvik could come back to find their houses had been looted." She sniffed. "Just like ours will be if we don't stop Thorbiorn!" She was trying not to cry.

"There must be some other way we can get in," Joe said, patting her shoulder awkwardly. "Thorbiorn's not here, so *he* must have thought of something else."

They both peered down at the ground.

"The tracks go this way." Lucy turned the horse to follow the prints that led along beside the city walls to the south-east.

As they trotted along, Joe turned the problem over in his mind. "What about the river?" he asked. "It must come in on one side of the city and go out on the other."

Lucy didn't reply at once.

"Does it go under the walls? Or what does it do?"

"No, it doesn't. But you're right," she said. "That's the answer. The river splits just to the south of the city, and there are no walls there at all because there's water all around."

"So if we cross the river just above where it splits, Jorvik is on the other side?"

She nodded.

After another minute or so, she brought the horse to a halt again. "That must be what Thorbiorn did," she said. "The tracks stop here."

Joe looked at the pulsing mass of water beside them in the darkness. The edge was fringed with ice, but a broad torrent flowed down the middle of the channel. It was black and sleek, but he knew that the speed and the numbing cold of the river would make it lethal.

"Look." Lucy pointed to a dark smear in the snow on the other side. "That's where they got out. The tracks pick up again over there."

"So, we ride the horse through the water?" Joe shivered. "How deep is it?"

"I don't know, but horses can swim. If Thorbiorn managed to get our horse to go across, I'm sure we can get this animal over to the other side."

"Isn't there anywhere shallower?"

Lucy shook her head.

"But we'll get wet!"

She shrugged. "Less wet than if we swim. And anyway, the current's too strong for us. We'd be swept away." She paused. "There's no other way, Joe. We have to do it."

Joe didn't answer.

"Are you ready then?" Lucy walked the horse forward. "Hold on tight to me. If the water comes up over the horse's back, lean into the current. If you fall off, I won't be able to save you."

"Right." He gulped. He thought of Mum and Dad. *I'm too young to die. It can't happen like this,* he thought. *Surely everything will be okay.* But he didn't believe it.

On the edge of the bank, the animal stopped and

whinnied.

"Come on, boy!" Lucy urged, digging her heels into its flanks. "Come on! You can do it!"

Joe wanted desperately to close his eyes, and not open them until they were on the other side. But he was afraid of losing his balance.

Tentatively, the horse edged towards the water. For one sickening second, its hooves slithered on the bank and it plunged downwards. Joe buried his face in Lucy's cloak.

Then it found its footing on the river bed and began to walk slowly forward. Icy water rushed into Joe's shoes and up his legs to his knees. He gasped. It felt like someone was beating the flesh of his feet and calves with the claw of a hammer. He couldn't remember the cold ever being this painful in all his life.

Lucy cajoled the horse onwards. As they reached the channel in the middle of the river, the water became even deeper. The beating sensation moved up Joe's thighs. He winced. He felt the horse stagger under the force of the current. If it lost its footing, he and Lucy would drown. He held on more tightly to her, as though clinging together would save them.

And then the beating on his legs began to recede. The horse was steadier beneath them. He peeped over Lucy's shoulder. With a final scramble, the animal struggled out on to the bank on the other side.

Joe heard Lucy let out her breath in a rush. "Well done, boy! You did it!" She bent over and hugged the neck of the horse.

"I can't believe it!" Joe cried. Despite the pain in his legs and feet, he felt jubilant. "We made it!" He gave Lucy a squeeze. "Well done!"

She turned round to look at him. Her face was alight with relief. "There was one moment where I thought ..." She left the sentence unfinished.

"I know. But it's okay. We're safe now."

She beamed. Then she gave herself a little shake. "We should get off and walk the horse the rest of the way to our house."

"Why?"

"Because we have to be ready for Thorbiorn. I don't know about you, but my feet are so numb, I think I might fall over when I try and stand on them."

Joe nodded. Stiffly, he swung one leg over the horse's back and lowered himself to the ground. As Lucy had predicted, his legs sank beneath him and he collapsed in the snow. "Aaagh! You're right! Ouch!"

Lucy clambered down beside him, grimacing as she crumpled to her knees.

"We'll never be able to take Thorbiorn on like this!" Joe giggled. "We're like a pair of jellyfish."

"It's not funny, you know!" she said, but still she started to laugh.

They lay on their backs in the snow, shaking

their hands and waggling their feet vigorously to try to get the blood moving again. Quickly, however, the cold began to seep through their cloaks.

"Come on!" Joe got to his feet, groaning. The pain of getting cold was nothing compared to the excruciating sensation of the feeling starting to come back in his fingers and toes. He made himself keep stamping his feet and rubbing his hands together.

Lucy took hold of the reins of the horse, who hadn't moved while they'd been lying on the ground. "Let's go, then." She flinched as she put her foot forward. Joe knew she was feeling the same pain as him.

The city was completely silent as they set off up the nearest street. The only sound they could hear was their own breath and the quiet crunching of their feet and the horse's hooves in the fresh snow. The tracks of Thorbiorn's horse lay ahead of them, but the white blanket which lay over everything was otherwise pristine.

"Something's different here," Joe muttered, aware of his voice breaking the hush.

"Well, it's all covered in snow." Lucy whispered. Her eyes danced with laughter.

"Not that! No, I know what it is. It's the smell. It's gone."

"What smell?"

"The rubbish and the smoke. I guess the rubbish is all frozen and covered over. But there's no smoke from any of the houses."

"Well, there's nobody here to tend the fires. Most people will have put theirs out like we did before we left."

They walked on without speaking until they came to the top of Coppergate. Outside Lucy's house stood the horse Thorbiorn had taken.

Joe's footsteps faltered. Beside him, he felt Lucy hesitate as well. Throughout their long, dark journey, he hadn't quite believed the older boy would actually be here. Even as they'd followed Thorbiorn's tracks along the outside of the city walls and through the streets, he'd told himself that they would be too late, or that they were following someone else altogether. But Thorbiorn was here, exactly as Lucy had feared.

"What shall we do?" Joe whispered.

"We have to go in. We have to stop him!"

"Do you have your knife?"

She stooped down and unfastened it from the cord that hung down beneath her pinafore.

"We don't have anything else, do we?"

She shook her head. "The only thing we have on our side is surprise," she murmured. "He won't be expecting us."

"Should we tie the horse up here? In case it whinnies or stamps or something."

"He'd probably assume it was the other horse, if he heard anything. But it might be best all the same." She unlooped one end of the reins and tethered the horse to a hook on the corner of the house beside them. "Remember," she whispered, "it's going to be pitch dark inside without the fire. I'm more used to feeling my way around in there, so I'll go first. You follow me, but stay close."

They tiptoed down the snowy street together, trying to keep their feet in the other horse's hoof prints to make as little sound as possible. At the house, they stopped. The door stood slightly open. From inside, came the muffled sound of someone moving around and cursing.

They looked at each other. On impulse, Joe reached out and squeezed Lucy's hand. She gave him a strained smile.

Then she turned back towards the house and pushed the door open.

16

The first thing that struck Joe as he peered over Lucy's shoulder was that the room beyond *wasn't* completely dark. Tiny flickering lights glowed in three different places. He frowned. One came from a small heap of curled wood shavings on the hearth, where the fire would usually be. But the other two were along the bottom of the walls. It was freezing, but there was a bitter smell in the air.

The room was even more bare than usual. For a moment, Joe thought that Thorbiorn had decided to steal much more than just the horn. Then he remembered that the cooking pot and its frame, and the cloths which usually hung on the walls, were all in the tent back at the encampment. So too were the fleeces for the earth sleeping benches and the trestle table.

Lucy stood motionless. At the far end of the room, Thorbiorn was crouching beside the back wall, hunched over something they couldn't see. He seemed not to have heard them open the door.

Joe touched Lucy's arm. She turned her head.

"What's he doing?" he mouthed.

She shook her head and made a face to say she didn't know. Then she pointed. On one of the earth benches lay a long, twisted stick with a sharp point at one end. It did look like how you would imagine a unicorn's horn, Joe thought.

Although the exchange between them had passed without a sound, Thorbiorn glanced over his shoulder. In a flash, he sprang to his feet, and whipped round to face them. His shadow leapt up on the wall behind him, towering monstrously over them all. A small flame flickered behind his feet.

"You two!" he snarled. "I should have known you'd turn up again!"

He advanced a few paces towards them.

"Unbelievable!" His eyes were narrow. "There's not another soul in the whole of Jorvik, but here we all are together! What are the chances of that?"

"What are you doing in our house?" Lucy asked through her teeth. She took a step into the room, her knife clasped tightly in her fist which was hidden behind her cloak.

"Me? I've come for what's rightfully mine!" His gaze flitted to the bench where the horn lay and then back to Lucy. "That's right!" He laughed grimly, relishing the expression on her face. "The horn that your uncle stole when he slaughtered my father!"

"He did not!" Lucy cried. "That's been in our

family for generations!"

"Oh yes? Is that what your father told you?"

She ignored his taunt and took another step forward. "How did you find it?"

The older boy smiled sweetly. "I looked for it, when I came in to see to your dogs!"

Joe saw Lucy's shoulders tense in front of him.

"I couldn't find it anywhere, so I thought perhaps you kept it somewhere else, away from the house. I did find this chest, though it was locked then." Thorbiorn looked down at the open lid of the box sunk in the ground beside his feet. "And the very next day, I heard you and your friend talking about the horn in the street. That was careless, don't you think? So I knew it must be in here. After that, it was just a matter of waiting for the right moment to steal the keys from your mother." He looked so pleased with himself, Joe wanted to punch him.

"She led me a merry dance this evening, I must say." Thorbiorn chuckled without mirth. "But I was patient, like a good boy. And this was my reward!" He gestured grandly at the chest. "I must admit, I was rather disappointed by how little else of value is in there. I was hoping there might be enough to pay my way to Dublin without starting to shave the end off the precious horn." He shrugged. "The silver plate will cover some of it, I suppose. The rest is barely worth the effort of carrying it."

"How dare you?" Lucy screeched. "Those are

my family's treasures!" All of a sudden, she flew at him, her knife held out in front of her.

Thorbiorn's hand went to his belt, but his own knife wasn't there. Surprise flashed across his face. Then he reached out and knocked Lucy's knife from her hand.

Before she could bend to pick it up, he caught hold of her wrist and twisted her arm behind her back. She yelped. He caught hold of her other arm, and pulled her roughly in front of him, holding her like a shield. Then in one fluid movement, he stepped sideways and seized the horn. He spun it round. The sharp point came up beneath her jaw.

"You move a muscle," he growled at Joe, "and I'll stab this into her throat so she bleeds like a stuck pig!"

Standing in the doorway, Joe tried desperately to think what to do. Lucy's knife was on the ground, but he doubted it would be much use, even if he could get it; Aileen had taken with her any knives she might use for cutting meat; and he could see Thorbiorn's knife down on the floor beside the back wall, well out of reach. In the meantime, the tiny lights along the walls had grown into knee-high flames, licking their way up the wattle. The air was filled with vile smelling smoke.

He quailed inwardly. There was no time to lose. Yet if he made a mistake, Lucy's prophecy about the unicorn's horn would come true - Thorbiorn would take it, leaving Lucy bleeding to death in a house which was burning down!

Joe took a deep breath. He had only one weapon: Thorbiorn's uncertainty. Just now, he couldn't see how to make use of it. But he had to do something.

He spread out his hands in front of him, as though to show he meant no harm. "Why are you doing that, Thorbiorn?" he asked, playing for time. "It's not her you want, is it? It's me. We both know that."

In the flickering light, he thought he saw confusion in the other boy's face.

"Twice, you've nearly done it," he said, hoping to sound encouraging.

"Yes!" Thorbiorn snapped. "And both times, you've got away, by some witchery or magic!"

Watching him, Joe realised with a small thrill that it wasn't confusion in Thorbiorn's eyes. It was fear.

Thorbiorn shifted his grip on Lucy. She stifled a sob. "If I let her go," he snarled, "and take you as my hostage, how do I know you won't vanish again?"

Joe nodded in agreement. He didn't know either.

Thorbiorn moved the point of the horn around Lucy's neck. She choked. The horn had caught on the chain of the St. Christopher. "What's this?" He leaned round from behind her to look at her throat.

Neither of them answered.

"Well? What is it?" Thorbiorn gave a little jab with the tip of the horn.

Lucy cried out.

"It's a lucky charm," Joe said quickly.

"Not so lucky now, is it?" Thorbiorn prised the chain away from her throat, and then with a flick of the horn, snapped it. The St. Christopher skittered across the floor towards the doorway.

Joe watched it. More than anything, he wanted to pick it up. The sight of it rolling along the ground reminded him overwhelmingly of home, or at least of being in York in his own time. But if he touched it, he might be whisked back into his own world, leaving Lucy at Thorbiorn's mercy.

"Joe gave it to me," Lucy said, biting back tears. "It was to protect me when he wasn't with me."

"How sweet! But now that he is, you don't need it, is that what you're saying?"

At that moment, inspiration tumbled into Joe's mind. "That's right," he said from the doorway, still not moving. "It calls me to her from wherever I am. You know already I can travel through time and space, just as I like. And when she wears that, I can take her with me." He leaned on the door frame, pretending that he was calm, and that his heart wasn't pounding in his chest. This had to work, he thought fiercely. It had to!

"How do you think we came to be here at the same time as you?" he asked.

Thorbiorn didn't reply.

"Now that you've broken the chain," Joe went

on, "I can't take her out of your grip." He smiled at Lucy, hoping to convey to her a confidence that he didn't feel. "But I can pick it up and use it to fetch Lokki."

He paused, to let Thorbiorn think about this.

"Let's just say," he continued, "that I bend down to pick it up. If you carry out your threat and drive the horn into her neck, I'll be back here with Lokki in just a few seconds." He watched Thorbiorn's face carefully. "Do you think he'll spare your life when he sees you've killed his daughter?"

Thorbiorn's eyes widened.

"Of course not!" Joe answered his own question. "He's a warrior! You'll be lucky if he gives you time to beg for mercy before he cuts your head off!"

He had barely finished speaking before Thorbiorn thrust Lucy away from him. He flung himself towards the doorway where Joe stood. Joe staggered backwards and fell.

Instinctively, he grabbed hold of Thorbiorn's cloak and locked his legs around the other boy. The horn was trapped between them. Its twisted edge ground painfully against Joe's ribs. He clenched every muscle, determined not to let Thorbiorn escape! The two boys rolled over and over, wrestling in the doorway for what seemed like an eternity.

Then there was a crack. Joe felt a searing pain in his side. For a split second, he loosened his hold on the older boy. Thorbiorn seized his chance, and threw himself over Joe and out into the street, still on his hands and knees. He scrabbled to his feet and lunged again at the doorway, grasping for the two pieces of horn that lay on the ground.

Summoning all his strength, Joe struck out with his foot, shoving Thorbiorn backwards. The other boy slipped, struggled to keep his balance in the snow, and then fell. Joe snatched the part of the horn with the sharp end. He lurched up on to his knees, brandishing it at Thorbiorn.

The older boy shimmied away like a crab making for a rock. Then he got slowly to his feet without taking his eyes off Joe. For a few seconds, he stood, tense and motionless, as though about to pounce again.

Suddenly, the silence was broken by the dull thudding of hooves galloping through the snow towards them.

Thorbiorn turned his head sharply and listened. Then he sprang away and up on to the back of the horse he'd left tethered by the house. He wrenched the rope free, screeching and beating the animal. The horse screamed and rose up on its hind legs. Thorbiorn clung on. Then it fled down the street with him still astride it, away from the sound of the oncoming hooves.

Joe slumped down in the doorway of Lucy's house. Something really hurt in his side.

"Are you alright?" Lucy's face looked down at

him.

"I think so," he muttered. "What about the fire? We need to do something before the whole house catches light."

Before she could answer, a huge horse, bigger even than the one they had ridden, came thundering down the street towards them. It reared up above their heads as it halted.

Lokki jumped down.

"Joe? Luiseach? What in the name of Valhalla are you doing here?"

Lucy ran forward and threw her arms around her father. "You came? How did you know? Oh Father, Joe was so brave! But Thorbiorn has taken our horse!"

Joe looked down at the pieces of horn. The one in his hand had blood on the snapped end. "I'm sorry," he said. "Your horn got broken. I know it was very valuable." He waited to see if Lokki was going to be angry. He felt weak.

"Thorbiorn has been trying to burn the house down!" Lucy cried. "I put out two of the fires with my cloak. I know it was new, but there were no buckets and no water." She pushed away from him. "There's one more I must put out."

Lokki shook his head in wonder as she disappeared into the house again. He stooped to Joe. "That's a nasty gash you've got there, boy."

Joe winced as Lokki lifted the material of his tunic and undershirt away from his skin. He looked down. A red rose of blood had spread through them from a deep wound in his side.

"I'm going to pack that with snow to stop the bleeding." Lucy's father had scooped up a handful of icy crystals and pressed them into the cut before Joe could even speak. He bit down hard on the edge of his tongue to stop himself from shouting out.

"Now then. Let's get inside, and then you can tell me what on earth has happened here." Lokki bent down and picked up the second piece of the horn from the ground. "At least this will fit more easily into the chest now!" His eyes twinkled.

He helped Joe to his feet and into the house. Lucy had put out the fires around the walls, but the flames Thorbiorn had conjured on the hearth leapt higher now. Lucy bent over them, feeding them with kindling from a basket.

As she worked, she told her father how they had seen Thorbiorn leaving the encampment, how they had taken someone else's horse and ridden through the night and found the gates closed, and then crossed the icy river. Finally, she told him what had happened when they arrived here.

Lokki sat on a stool warming his hands at the fire and listening while he looked around the room. The ragged ends of burned willow still smoked around the holes in the walls, and the planks lay askew across the floor where Thorbiorn had kicked them aside to uncover the chest in the ground.

"He'd obviously planned it carefully," Lokki said at last. "Even setting light to the house. He must have realised there would be no fire anywhere and brought a fire steel with him specially." He scratched his chin. "It's quite different from what I feared, you know. I owe you both a huge debt, especially you, Joe."

"What did you think had happened?" Lucy asked.

"Well, your mother discovered her keys were gone. She hoped they'd fallen off back at the tent, but when she and Mattheus went to fetch the shovels for the burial, they found that you children and the horse had gone, too. Mattheus came running back to tell me." He rubbed his forehead. "I feel ashamed now. But I thought it must be you, Joe. I thought perhaps you *had* killed the dogs somehow, since they were so afraid of you, and now you'd stolen Aileen's keys, taken my daughter, and used my horse to ride back here and steal the narwhal horn."

"Narwhal?" Lucy looked up, stricken. "So Joe was right? It's not from a unicorn! What about the curse?"

"What curse?"

Lucy chanted the words she'd recited to Joe.

Lokki grinned broadly. "Who told you that? Your older brother? You don't want to believe everything he says! We'd *say* the horn was from a unicorn if we traded with it abroad. That's what makes it so valuable, you see. But any seafarer worth his salt knows it comes from the Arctic waters. The prophecy is obviously Mattheus' little joke. Now then, don't look so crestfallen!" He reached out and stroked her arm. "Anyway, I borrowed the fastest horse I could, and followed you back. I had to cross the river too, just like you." He looked down absent-mindedly at his sodden boots.

"Don't you want to go after Thorbiorn?" Joe asked after a few moments. "He left less than a minute before you got here. You'd catch him up easily."

"Did he say where he was going?"

"Dublin, I think. He wanted to use the horn to pay his way."

Lokki shrugged. "He's got the horse, I suppose. But that won't get him far. All the same, I doubt he'll come back here because he knows he'll be punished for the theft and the fire." He looked ruefully at the smoke in the air. "You know, I think I'd prefer it if I never saw him again, rather than haul him back to face his punishment. That will only stoke his fury and his desire for revenge."

Lucy looked at the two pieces of horn between Lokki's feet. "Did my uncle steal the horn from Thorbiorn's father when he killed him? That's what Thorbiorn said."

Lokki picked up the pieces and turned them round in his hands. "No. My father definitely had it when I was a child." He fitted the pieces together. "I'll repair it if I can. Then maybe I'll borrow Cousin Finwith's horse and ride out of the Danelaw when the better weather comes. I'm sure I can sell some of the powder to those scruffy people further south. They'll believe it's from a unicorn, so I should make enough to pay for the repairs to the house and a new horse for us."

Lucy straightened up and went to pick up the St. Christopher from the floor. "I'm sorry the chain got broken," she said, holding it out to Joe. "But I think it did its job, keeping me safe. It's time for you to have it back."

Joe hesitated. He didn't know whether the St. Christopher would take him home, or whether he wanted to go. Part of him yearned to be warm and dry again, and to be rid of the pain in his side. But another part wanted to see the rest of Lucy's family return, to enjoy a few moments of glory, and to be here still when they'd sold some of the horn and mended their house. Perhaps they might even spend some of the money on a few luxuries to make their lives a little less hard. He hoped so.

Lucy smiled at him. "You did say you wanted it back in the end. Here, take it."

Slowly, Joe stretched out his hand.

As his fingers closed over the little silver disk, the familiar rushing sound filled his ears.

"By the way," he heard Lucy say,"was it true, what you told Thorbiorn about using it to carry people with you through time?" Her voice seemed to come from a great distance.

He shook his head and grinned. But the dizziness was suddenly too much. He shook his head again, harder this time, trying to stop it. He couldn't! He grasped around with his hands for something to hold on to. He hadn't said goodbye to her. He wasn't ready! Just a minute more!

"Are you alright, Joe?"

His head was swimming. He tried to focus. His teacher was standing at the front of the classroom, her pen in her hand. She was looking at him strangely.

"Yes, thanks. I'm fine," he mumbled, and promptly fainted on to his desk.

"It's not like you to pass out like that," his mother said, as she patted the duvet down around him back at home, half an hour later. "Is this what happened with Dad on York station?"

"I don't know," Joe said truthfully.

"Well, I'll take you to see the doctor as soon as I can get an appointment." She stood up. "I'll be back up in a minute with a drink for you."

Joe snuggled down beneath the covers. It was wonderful to be somewhere warm and comfortable again. He knew there was nothing wrong with him, except that he really was as tired as if he'd been up all night.

He waited until he could hear Mum in the kitchen, then pulled up his pyjama top and peered under the duvet at the place on his side where the horn had stabbed him. As he'd guessed, there was no blood and no scab. But he could just make out a very faint v-shape on his skin where scar tissue had formed.

He pulled his top down again and settled back on his pillows, satisfied. The St. Christopher was still in the pocket of his trousers, where he'd managed to hide it before Mum saw it. All he had to do now was find a way of buying another new chain. In fact, perhaps he should buy two, just in case it got broken again next time he was in Lucy's world.

Next time. He closed his eyes. Where would that be? Not Jorvik, he was fairly sure. He might not have said goodbye to her, but he had a feeling that his time there was over. Clearly, it wouldn't be Fishbourne either.

He wondered idly about going to the library to see what bit of history came next after the Vikings. Then he decided that he wouldn't. There wasn't much point really, since he didn't know how many hundreds of years he would have to skip to get to the right time.

For now, anyway, it was good just to be home for a bit. His own world was so much easier to live in than hers.

And when the chance did come to slip into

another time again, it would be a nice surprise. It would be hard work, he knew that now, and probably quite dangerous. But at least it would be an adventure.

Of that, he was absolutely certain.

WANT TO READ ON?

Try the next book in
***The Scar Gatherer* series …**

The Falconer's Quarry

Chapter 1

Joe was out riding with Sam when it happened. In fact, they'd only just set off.

"Aren't you coming with us?" he'd asked Dad, as they stood in the stable yard.

Dad grinned. "No thanks. I'll wait here. An hour in the sunshine with a newspaper sounds perfect to me!"

The lady from the stables approached. "I'm afraid we've got a bit of a problem. I'd booked you boys in for two of my beginners' horses, but one of them's looking a bit lame." She scratched her head. "My others are already out this morning. I do have a horse tacked up for someone who didn't come, but he can be a bit frisky, so I normally only use him for people who've ridden before."

"I have," Joe said.

The lady brightened. "How many hours, would you say?"

Joe thought about it. There had been a few lessons with Heraclio at Fishbourne last summer, and then in February the long ride back to Jorvik across the snowy wastes, after the ship burial. "Four or five, I guess. Perhaps a bit more."

His brother turned on him. "When?"

Joe shuffled his feet. "When you weren't there," he mumbled.

The lady considered. "It's not much, but we should be okay." She strode over to one of the sheds and took down a pair of riding hats from the hooks. "Let's get going, then."

Dad waved cheerfully to Joe and Sam as they rode out of the gate and onto the bridle path. "I should have brought the camera!" he called after them. "You look great!"

Joe beamed. Dad had let each of them choose a particular activity while they were away on holiday together this time, and riding had been Joe's choice. It felt good to be up on a horse again, and much more comfortable with the saddle and stirrups than it had been bareback behind Lucy. He pressed his heels into the horse's flanks experimentally. Immediately, the animal sped up and overtook Sam's horse.

"You seem to have a good seat," the lady said as he drew level with her, "though you're holding the reins a bit strangely. Keep them like this," she nodded at her own hands, "like I showed your brother. That's better. You can go ahead if you like. But don't let the horse run away with you! You're in charge, remember!"

Joe shifted his grip on the reins and dug his heels in a little more. The horse began to trot. Joe realised that he had settled naturally into the correct rhythm on the animal's back. That was what Heraclio had been trying to get him to do. He'd found it difficult, the way you had to go up and down much more slowly than if you let the horse bounce you. Mind you, that beast had been single-minded about throwing him off whenever it could.

He urged the horse on a little more. It responded at once, speeding up and changing gait. Cantering was so much better, Joe thought. It felt fast and smooth. He gave a very quiet whoop of delight, not wanting to frighten the animal.

"At the bottom of the slope, we're going to go right!" called the lady from behind him. "Don't get too far ahead, please!"

All at once, Joe began to panic. The end of the track was coming towards him rather quickly now, and he couldn't remember how to slow down or steer. Now that he thought about it, he wasn't even sure he knew. Lucy had held the reins last time. She had controlled the horse. All he'd had to do was stay on!

He tugged the leather straps he was holding. The horse shied, confused. Joe realised he was digging his feet into its flanks, so he was urging the animal on at the same time as he was pulling it back. He made himself relax his legs. It felt precarious, but the horse slowed down. Joe let his breath whistle out between his teeth. Tentatively, he pulled the right-hand rein. The horse turned towards the right and started along the next part of the route. Joe grinned. He could do this. It was going to be fine.

As the horse walked along in the April sunshine, Joe became aware of a buzzing sound nearby. It grew abruptly very loud, and then just as suddenly stopped. He looked around, wondering what it might be. Crawling up the horse's shoulder was a giant wasp.

Alarm tightened Joe's throat. He'd never seen such a huge wasp in his life! It was almost as long as his thumb and a sort of reddish brown rather than yellow.

He swallowed. It wasn't a wasp. It must be a hornet!

Slowly, he turned in his saddle. The lady from the stables was still some way off up the track with Sam. If he shouted to them, the hornet might get angry and sting the horse.

But he was going to have to do something. Otherwise, it would crawl up on to his knee and sting him! His whole body tensed. The horse pricked up its ears and shook its mane, sensing his anxiety.

Joe shifted the reins to his left hand. He would have to brush the hornet off and hope he didn't aggravate it too much. He gritted his teeth. There was only going to be one chance at this. He leaned forward and flicked the horse's shoulder with the leather strap.

The horse started in surprise. The hornet rose up, buzzing furiously. It disappeared into the horse's ear.

There was a moment of quiet. Then the animal screamed and reared up on its hind legs, flailing its hooves.

Joe grabbed handfuls of mane and clung on desperately. He could feel himself sliding down its back. He clenched his knees to the saddle.

The horse jerked its head frantically up and down. The hornet flew out.

Before Joe had time to catch hold of the reins, the horse had lunged forward and bolted down the path.

Faster and faster they went. Joe found himself standing in the stirrups, bent forward like a jockey. All he could think of was not falling off.

The horse galloped onwards, its ears flat back against its head. Fields flew past on either side. Then they were speeding along the edge of a copse.

Joe looked up over the horse's head. Across the track in front of them was a five-bar gate.

The horse saw it too.

It tried to stop. But it was too late.

At the last moment, it veered off the track into the copse.

Joe was flung one way, then the other. A branch swooped into his face. He ducked low and threw up his arm. Still the horse careered through the trees.

And then without warning, Joe was flying through the air. His fingers were free of the horse's tangled hair, his limbs spread wide like a star. For one eternal second, everything was peaceful.

Then he hit the ground with a rib-crunching smack.

The world went dark.

When he sat up, he didn't know whether a few seconds had passed, or several minutes. He groaned. He felt sick and his head throbbed.

The woodland around him was dim, though there were patches of sunlight on the ground here and there. He rubbed his face with his hands and peered through the trees. He couldn't see the track. The wood just stretched on and on, with no sign of fields beyond.

Perhaps he was looking the wrong way. He could well have got disorientated by the bump he'd just had. He swivelled painfully round. But there was no sign of open ground between the trees in any direction.

He frowned. He'd thought the woodland had been lighter than this, beeches and birches not yet fully in leaf. But overhead now were mostly fir trees, with the occasional oak among them.

He could feel his brain struggling to get a message through to him. But it was like being underwater, hearing sounds that he couldn't make out. As the muddle began to clear, he looked down at himself.

He caught his breath sharply. His clothes had completely changed! The horse had thrown him not just to the ground, but into another time! His stomach churned. *Not now!* he wanted to shout. *I'm not ready for this! My ribs hurt. My head hurts. Everything hurts!*

THE FIRST BOOK IN The Scar Gatherer SERIES
THE LEOPARD IN THE GOLDEN CAGE
JULIA EDWARDS

THE SECOND BOOK IN The Scar Gatherer SERIES
SAVING THE UNICORN'S HORN
JULIA EDWARDS

THE FALCONER'S QUARRY
JULIA EDWARDS

HAVE YOU READ THEM ALL?

THE DEMON IN THE EMBERS
JULIA EDWARDS

THE FIFTH BOOK IN The Scar Gatherer SERIES
SLAVES FOR THE ISABELLA
JULIA EDWARDS

THE SIXTH BOOK IN The Scar Gatherer SERIES
THE SHIMMER ON THE GLASS
JULIA EDWARDS

THE RING FROM THE RUINS
JULIA EDWARDS

Lightning Source UK Ltd.
Milton Keynes UK
UKHW011955261120
374145UK00001B/124

9 780992 844325